WATSON DOES NOT LIE

A CHRONOLOGY OF SHERLOCK HOLMES AND JOHN H. WATSON

WATSON DOES NOT LIE

A CHRONOLOGY OF SHERLOCK HOLMES AND JOHN H. WATSON

PAUL THOMAS MILLER

WILDSIDE PRESS

With many thanks to my wife Karen for her patience with my Holmesmania and to Margie Deck and Mattias Boström for their considerable help with this project.

CONTENTS

INTRODUCTION

I was told the creation of a Holmesian Chronology is practically a rite of passage. I was told once you have managed to make sense of the sixty stories you emerge a rookie no more. I was told it is a task that improves you and your understanding of The Canon.

I'm not so sure. I think it would be better to warn that as you value your life and your reason, you should keep away from the dates.

I found myself dissatisfied with chronologies I read. Too many chronologists resorted to claiming either Watson lied, or could not read his own notes. Such ideas are scandalous. I wanted a chronology built upon the idea of Watson's words as facts. Since I could not find one, I created one.

Chronologies tend to make for clunky and stodgy reading. I've tried to avoid this by presenting my arguments as simply and lightly as possible.

The text is divided into two parts. The first part presents my arguments for the dating of each case. The dates I give create a complicated marital history for Dr. John H. Watson; therefore, a discussion of the many wives of Watson is included.

The second part is comprised of two lists: firstly, a brief list of the principal action in the sixty canonical stories—essentially putting the Canon in order; secondly, a long chronology of all dates I have isolated in the Canon. I made the long list up of as many dates and times as possible, including any calculable marriages, birth dates and other histories of people in The Canon.

With my mind irretrievably shattered by the twistings of logic required to create it, I present my chronology…

Paul Thomas Miller

MY PREMISES

AN OUTLINE OF THE RULES GOVERNING THE CHRONOLOGY

I created this chronology to meet my personal expectations of Watson's work. As such, I approached it using several premises which I hold to be true and inviolable. These are presented in order of importance.

1. Watson does not lie.

Many chronologies argue when a case does not fit where the chronologists want it, Watson must be telling a lie. "Wisteria Lodge" is a prime example: simply because the date Watson gives lies in the period Holmes was supposed dead, they assume Watson lied to them.

At best these "errors" are explained by the nonsense he misread his own writing. We know he took copious notes of his doings with Holmes and we know he did this so he could write the stories later. As he was not a blithering idiot, he would have made notes he knew he could read later. Indeed, he proudly makes a point about his fastidious note-keeping when he tells us the story of his time at Baskerville Hall: "I will follow the course of events by transcribing my own letters to Mr. Sherlock Holmes which lie before me on the table. One page is missing, but otherwise they are exactly as written and show my feelings and suspicions of the moment more accurately than my memory, clear as it is upon these tragic events, can possibly do." We can dismiss the notion of inadequate notes easily enough.

To my mind, the idea of Watson being an outright liar is even worse. Time and again Holmes points out what a poor liar Watson is. Frequently, when Holmes needs to lie to a client, he lies to Watson as well, because he knows Watson will be unable to keep up the pretence if he knows the truth. We see it in "The Retired Colourman" when Josiah Amberley is lured away to an Essex village, when Holmes sets himself up secretly on the moor in *The Hound of the Baskervilles*, and in "The Dying Detective" when it is imperative that Culverton Smith believe Holmes to be dying. To be sure, is there any greater example of this than Holmes allowing Watson to believe that he had died at the Reichenbach Falls? Holmes is not entirely heartless. He confesses he wanted to tell Watson the truth, but he could not because he knew it would jeopardise the secret.

And Holmes was right; when Watson does lie, he is terrible at it. On those occasions when Watson has to be dishonest in The Canon, he tells us he is going to do so. In "Charles Augustus Milverton," for example, Watson begins "…with due suppression the story may be told in such fashion as to injure no one… The reader will excuse me if I conceal the date or any other fact by which he might trace the actual occurrence." And yet you will see later on how easy it is to crack the mystery of dating the case. The same happens in "The Three Students." Watson tells us he is going to hide the location of the story and then does a dreadful job of it.

No, Watson does not lie. It is contrary to his nature. The things he tells us happened must have happened. If Watson's reports cause us problems in creating a chronology of the events, the solutions must be found elsewhere.

2. Holmes does lie. (And so do others.)

Of course, we should be careful not to confuse Watson lying with Watson believing a lie and passing it on. As we have seen, Holmes frequently tells Watson lies intentionally in order to have them passed on to others. Other characters in their adventures do the same or sometimes pass on information inaccurately. Some are not very good at getting their facts straight. Some are downright dishonest. As we go through The Canon, then, we do not have to believe *everything* we read, just that Watson is presenting the events as they happened to him.

3. We do not know how many wives Watson had.

Too many chronologists start from the premise Mary Watson was either Watson's only wife or, at best, one of two or three. There is no evidence for this. It is a dangerous assumption because the dates simply do not fit with this belief and the chronologist is forced to change dates which Watson is very clear about. Holmes explains this folly best in "A Scandal in Bohemia" when he says "It is a capital mistake to theorize before one has data. Insensibly one begins to twist facts to suit theories, instead of theories to suit facts." In my chronology I let the cases rest where they should, and I examined the question of Watson's wives afterwards.

That said, dating several of the cases involved identifying whether or not Watson was married. I dealt with all other cases first and then based my conclusions on the timeline of Watson's marital status. The details of Watson's marriages are considered in a separate section of the text.

4. When you have eliminated the impossible, whatever remains, however improbable, must be the truth.

A few of my conclusions may seem somewhat unlikely. For example, the facts regarding the events surrounding Wisteria Lodge. However, the master's maxim holds true: "when you have eliminated the impossible whatever remains, however improbable, must be the truth." I am confident that I have done just this.

5. Watson published privately.

Some of the cases were published privately by Watson in volumes we have yet to discover. This is proven in the second story. *The Sign of the Four* takes place four months before the first known publication of *A Study in Scarlet*, and yet in it, Watson tells us he has already "embodied it in a small brochure with the somewhat fantastic title of *A Study in Scarlet*." The only possible conclusion is that Watson published some of these stories privately before the known public versions came out. Most likely these were produced in very small runs for friends and other interested parties. This goes a long way to clearing up many of the accusations of inaccuracy in Watson's writing.

6. Watson made it clear when he was not writing from personal experience.

Several people have addressed the question of who wrote "His Last Bow," "The Mazarin Stone," and the second half of *A Study in Scarlet* because they are written from an unusual third person perspective. For many, the obvious fact is they were written by someone other than Watson and, therefore, they are not to be trusted. But there is nothing so deceptive as an obvious fact.

These stories *were* all written by Watson. However, he makes it clear when he is not reporting from personal experience by turning to the third person. It is his way of letting us know that while the facts are accurate to the best of his knowledge, that knowledge is second hand and may be liable to error.

7. The original text is the proper text.

Several of the stories have been tampered with since their original publication. For example, in "The Five Orange Pips" the original text has Watson's wife staying with her mother, whereas some later versions change this to her aunt. I stand firm: the original text is what Watson wrote and what Watson meant. And deviations from this text are due to outside forces tampering with The Canon. Most likely they felt they were correcting errors, but in my view, they were simply muddying the waters. That said, there is one exception—"The Musgrave Ritual"—in which the original text is unquestionably in error, missing two vital lines of the ritual itself.

8. The Great Hiatus dates.

I take the dates of The Great Hiatus (that period when Holmes was presumed dead at the bottom of the Reichenbach Falls until his miraculous return in "The Empty House") to be exactly as indicated by Watson: from 04 May 1891 to 01 April 1894.

.THE ADVENTURES

THE DATE OF EACH ADVENTURE, THE DIFFICULTIES ENCOUNTERED IN PLACING EACH ONE ON A CHRONOLOGICAL TIMELINE, AND THE SOLUTIONS TO THOSE DIFFICULTIES

A Study in Scarlet (*STUD*)

First publicly published: November 1887

Main action (Part I): 04 March 1881 to 05 March 1881

Main action (Part II): 04 May 1847 to 1865

The Battle of Maiwand—in which Watson was injured—took place on 27 July 1880. Given Watson's account of the events from the Battle of Maiwand onwards, it is not difficult to work out that "the 4th of March" on which Holmes becomes involved in the Lauriston Garden case is 04 March 1881. From there, working out all of the other dates for Holmes and Watson's part in this story is straightforward.

The only difficulty is presented by an issue of *The Standard* which they read from on 05 March 1881. It states Stangerson and Drebber left their boarding house on 04 March 1881 when, in reality, they must have left it on 03 March 1881 (the day of the first murder). The reporting error must be due to sloppy journalism on the part of *The Standard*, a style which is held up by the British press to this day.

John Ferrier's story is easy to date because we are given 04 May 1847 as the day he and Lucy were found in the Great Alkali Plain.

The Jefferson Hope section of the story is possible to date thanks to the Mormons handily dating the grave of John Ferrier after they murdered him. Knowing he died 04 August 1860 means we can follow their adventures backwards and arrive at 13 June 1860 for the date Jefferson Hope proposed to Lucy Ferrier and then leaves, planning to return for her in two months. Sadly, we also know that Jefferson and Lucy met for the first time that same month. I have dated this meeting as 01 June 1860 to give them the maximum amount of time to fall in love ardently enough to warrant Jefferson's later fixation on revenge.

Incidentally, there is much debate among scholars as to where the facts of Part II—*The Country of the Saints*—came from. Jefferson Hope gives a brief indication before he is arrested and dies in his cell, but that does not provide enough for the full account we are given.

It should be remembered Jefferson had an assistant in his plot: the young man who posed as an old woman to retrieve Lucy's ring. It is reasonable to assume Jefferson told the young man his story and that is why he agreed to help. Tracking this man down after the event would pose no great difficulty to Sherlock Holmes. This man supplied the missing details. Perhaps there was a diary Hope left in his care. The credit is never given to the unnamed young man, of course, in fulfilment of a promise to keep him out of it, lest the police take an interest in him. Watson then wrote the account up in the third person, to indicate it was not his own experience.

The Sign of the Four (*SIGN*)

First publicly published: February 1890

Main action: 07 July 1888 to 10 July 1888

During her initial consultation with Holmes, Mary Morstan tells us "About six years ago—to be exact, upon the 4th of May, 1882—an advertisement appeared…" which puts the action firmly in 1888. She then refers to a letter which she received that morning postmarked 07 July. As the letter appears to have been posted and received the same day, we arrive at a starting date of 07 July 1888 from which all other dates may be easily deduced.

One difficulty this date presents for chronologists is the number of pearls Mary has received since May 1882. If she received one that year and every year since, as she says, she should now have seven pearls. However, when she shows Holmes and Watson the box containing them and the addresses which were on them, there are only six of each. The solution is obvious. When she received the first pearl, she had no reason to think the gift would be repeated. The mystery was not so great she felt the need to keep the address label, and a single pearl was of such little use that she thought nothing of selling it. It was only when the second pearl arrived, she began her collection.

Small's story is easy to roughly place, too. We know when the Indian Rebellion started and ended. Therefore, we have a time frame for Small being at Fort Agra. The only difficulty in his testimony is he says "three or four years ago, we found ourselves in England. I had no great difficulty in finding where Sholto lived," which would be 1884–5. However, we learn elsewhere Sholto died because he saw Small's face at the window in 1882, so he should have said "six years ago." This is no great obstacle. Small made a mistake. Given all he has been through, it is no great wonder he struggles to keep track of the years. Watson reports exactly what Small said, mistakes and all.

A Scandal in Bohemia (*SCAN*)

First publicly published: July 1891

Main action: 20 March 1888 to 22 March 1888

Dating this case is as easy as reading the story. Watson tells us very clearly that "it was on the twentieth of March, 1888."

Difficulties rise for chronologists who note he also says "I had seen little of Holmes lately. My marriage had drifted us away from each other." Given that he won't meet Mary Morstan for another four months, how can he be married to her? The short answer is: he cannot!

Watson says he is married, but he does not say he is married to Mary Morstan. Impossibilities eliminated, the truth (which some find improbable) is that Watson had at least one wife before Mary Morstan. In fact, as I show in a later section, Watson had a good many more marriages.

The Red-Headed League (*REDH*)

First publicly published: August 1891

Main action: 27 June 1890

The date of this case is easily calculated from the paper in which "The Red-Headed League" advertised their vacancy: "It is *The Morning Chronicle* of April 27, 1890." Jabez Wilson tells us it was shown to him by Spaulding who "came down into the office just this day eight weeks, with this very paper in his hand." The case, then, is brought to Holmes exactly eight weeks after the advert appears; that is, 27 June 1890.

Two objections may be raised to this date, but both are easily dealt with.

Firstly, we are told at the start of the story Watson called on Holmes "one day in the autumn of last year" but June is very much a summer month. This is a problem caused by Watson's florid style of writing. He meant the weather was autumnal, not the day was literally in autumn. He meant the weather was drearier than one would expect in June. This is an annoying trait of Watson's and it is no isolated incident. Indeed, I am inclined to agree with Holmes's sentiments in "The Retired Colourman" when he says "Cut out the poetry, Watson."

Secondly, the sign Jabez finds on the door of the offices on 27 June 1890 says "The Red-headed League is Dissolved October 9, 1890." Why this spurious date? We cannot know for certain, but I think this was a ploy designed to further confuse Jabez Wilson. Perhaps the hope was he would feel disorientated and put off investigations into the League for a few days. We do know Watson indicated the real date to us and reported the sign accurately. It is the sign which is incorrect, not Watson's account.

A Case of Identity (*IDEN*)

First publicly published: September 1891

Main action: 17 March 1890 to 18 March 1890

In "The Red-Headed League" Mary Sutherland's case is mentioned as having taken place "the other day." "A Case of Identity" must occur before "The Red-Headed League," but as close to it as possible.

Mary Sutherland's announcement in the *Saturday Chronicle* says Hosmer Angel went missing "on the morning of the fourteenth," which would be the wedding day. As the wedding day was the day before the announcement, we now also know it was a Friday. We need to look for a Friday the 14th as close as possible to "The Red-Headed League," which gives us 14 March 1890 or 14 February 1890. As March is closer, it is the more likely choice.

Mary describes how she waited for a few days before contacting Holmes, but she surely would not have stewed any longer than the weekend, so she consulted Holmes on Monday 17 March 1890. Once we have this date, the rest are easy to figure out.

The Boscombe Valley Mystery (*BOSC*)

First publicly published: October 1891

Main action: 06 June 1889 to 07 June 1889

We can immediately narrow the year of this case to between 1881 (when Holmes and Watson met) and 1891 (the publication date of this story).

Telling Watson about the crime, Holmes says "On June 3rd, that is, on Monday last, McCarthy left his house at Hatherley..." The only year in the correct range with a Monday 03 June is 1889. This rather neatly gives us the date of the crime as 03 June 1889.

After the first day's investigation goes against James McCarthy, Alice Turner recruits Inspector Lestrade to investigate on James's behalf. Lestrade arrives the following day and investigates, but the results are not to her liking. On the third day that Holmes is called in by Alice and Lestrade. Thus, Holmes's involvement commences on 06 June 1889.

The *Monmouthshire Beacon* of 20 July 1889 provides the date of the Herefordshire summer assizes. James McCarthy was cleared of all charges when they opened on 15 July 1889.

The Five Orange Pips (*FIVE*)

First publicly published: November 1891

Main action: Late September 1887

Watson states early on this is an 1887 case, when he tells us how busy a year it was. He follows this by saying "It was in the latter days of September" that Watson was staying with Holmes because his wife was staying with her mother.

People often question how Mary Morstan could be staying with her mother when we are told in *The Sign of the Four* her parents are both dead. The question is a mistake resulting from the assumption Mary Morstan is the wife in question—a clear case of twisting facts to suit theory. As a result, some subsequent reprints of the story are altered, substituting aunt for mother. Such fact-fiddling is unnecessary and reprehensible. The dates make this quite clear—Watson had not even met Mary Morstan yet. This must be a different wife.

The Man with the Twisted Lip (*TWIS*)

First publicly published: December 1891

Main action: 15 June 1889 to 20 June 1889

The date of this story is laid out clearly in the story. Near the start Watson tells us "it was in June, '89." Soon thereafter he is in an opium den talking to Isa Whitney who asks Watson what day it is. Watson replies "...Friday, June 19th," giving us the date of 19 June 1889 to work the rest around.

The immediate difficulty is 19 June 1889 was actually a Wednesday. However, bearing in mind Watson is trying to get a drugged-up Isa home quickly and easily, reconsider this part of their conversation:

> "I say, Watson, what o'clock is it?"
> "Nearly eleven."
> "Of what day?"
> "Of Friday, June 19th."
> "Good heavens! I thought it was Wednesday. It is Wednesday. What d'you want to frighten a chap for?"

As it *is* Wednesday, not Friday, Watson is merely attempting to put the fear up Isa Whitney to make him more easily managed. Perhaps this challenges my premise that Watson never lies. I accept it as a rare white lie. The fib attempts to deceive Isa for his own good. It is not a lie to *us*; he is telling *us* exactly what took place.

If anything, this lie backs up my premise Watson is no natural liar. He does a terrible job of fibbing, and Isa guesses exactly what is going on despite being doped out of his mind.

The Adventure of the Blue Carbuncle (*BLUE*)

First publicly published: January 1892

Main action: 27 December 1890

Watson tells us he "had called upon my friend Sherlock Holmes upon the second morning after Christmas" leaving us the year to figure out.

In conversation with Holmes, we learn that among the last six cases Watson was involved with are Holmes's "attempt to recover the Irene Adler papers,… the singular case of Miss Mary Sutherland, and… the adventure of the man with the twisted lip." Therefore we are looking for the first December after "A Scandal in Bohemia," "A Case of Identity," and "The Man with the Twisted Lip." The date, then, is 27 December 1890.

The Adventure of the Speckled Band (*SPEC*)

First publicly published: February 1892

Main action: 05 April 1883 to 06 April 1883

This adventure starts by giving us most of the date: "It was early in April in the year '83 that I woke one morning to find Sherlock Holmes standing, fully dressed, by the side of my bed."

Tracking the day down is slightly more difficult. Fortunately, Watson tells us when they got to Stoke Moran "It was a perfect day, with a bright sun and a few fleecy clouds in the heavens." When we look at the reports of the local weather in Saturday editions of *The Surrey Advertiser* for the first two weeks of April 1883, there is only one day which fits the bill. That is Thursday 5th April which was bright with only a slight mist.

The Adventure of the Engineer's Thumb (*ENGR*)

First publicly published: March 1892

Main action: 29 June 1889 to 30 June 1889

Watson tells us that this story takes place "in the summer of '89, not long after my marriage" but it is possible to narrow the date down further.

The action of the case takes place in "Eyford, in Berkshire. It is a little place near the borders of Oxfordshire, and within seven miles of Reading." Eyford is, of course, a poorly disguised Twyford—a village in the county of Berkshire about seven miles out of Reading.

On the morning after he loses his thumb, Victor Hatherley says "a bright morning was breaking when I came to myself." He then realises he is close to Eyford Station. He converses with the station master who tells him the next train is due within an hour. Then he gets on the train and arrives at Paddington Station at 6 am.

By consulting a train timetable for Twyford to Paddington in 1850 (unfortunately, the closest in date I could find) I discovered the trip would take about one hour and fifteen minutes. This means he boarded the train at 4:45 am. If we assume he took ten minutes to come to his senses and then get to the station and another forty-five conversing and waiting for the train, we can deduce "a bright morning was breaking" at about 3:50 am. Sunrise in the Reading area on 30 June 1889 was indeed at 3:50 am, giving us the date of this case.

There is room for error here in the train journey time and how long it took him from waking to boarding the train, but, as Holmes warned Watson, we must not be too timid in our inferences.

The Adventure of the Noble Bachelor (*NOBL*)

First publicly published: April 1892

Main action: 14 October 1887

While looking up their client, Holmes reads "Lord Robert Walsingham de Vere St. Simon… Born in 1846." and from this deduces "He's forty-one years of age." This means the year is 1887.

Watson tells us that it is "a few weeks before my own marriage, during the days when I was still sharing rooms with Holmes in Baker Street." Comparing this with the marital history of Watson (discussed later in this book), we are brought to October 1887.

Holmes deduces from Francis H. Moulton's receipt dated 04 October that the bill was settled "within a week." This puts the wedding within seven days of that date. Additionally, a newspaper report Holmes reads from a paper dated "Wednesday last" indicates the wedding took place the previous day. Therefore, we know the wedding took place on a Tuesday within a week of 04 October.

The date of the wedding must be 11 October 1887. The rest of the dates flow easily from there.

The Adventure of the Beryl Coronet (*BERY*)

First publicly published: May 1892

Main action: 09 February 1884 to 10 February 1884

As the story begins with Holmes and Watson living together on "a bright, crisp February morning," we are immediately limited to Februarys between the pair meeting and the publication date of this story. These are 1882 to 1891, inclusive (1892 may be discounted as it occurs during The Great Hiatus).

From these we may eliminate 1888, 1889, and 1891 as Watson is married and not living at 221b.

We may also eliminate 1890, as this is a year for which (as noted in "The Final Problem") Watson only has notes for three cases. We already know these cases are "A Case of Identity," "The Blue Carbuncle," and "The Red-Headed League."

On the first day of his involvement in the case Watson reports "the snow of the day before still lay deep upon the ground." Looking at the monthly Meteorological Office reports for the remaining years, only one meets the requirements: 10 February 1884 when there was "even in London wet snow on the morning, of the 10th."

With this date found, the rest of the case can be placed easily.

The Adventure of the Copper Beeches (*COPP*)

First publicly published: June 1892

Main action: March 1891

I can only narrow this case down to a month and year.

Spring is usually the months of March, April, and May, so from "It was a cold morning of the early spring" we can deduce Watson means March; the early part of spring.

In conversation with Holmes, Watson says "You remember that the affair of the blue carbuncle..." Meaning the events of "The Blue Carbuncle" (in December 1890) had already taken place. We are limited to 1891 and 1892. With 1892 in The Great Hiatus, the events of "The Copper Beeches" must find themselves in March 1891.

The Adventure of Silver Blaze (*SILV*)

First publicly published: December 1892

Main action: 02 April 1891 to 07 April 1891

Holmes informs Watson he has "made a blunder, my dear Watson—which is, I am afraid, a more common occurrence than any one would think who only knew me through your memoirs." This reference to the public knowing Holmes through Watson's memoirs (plural) indicates at least two stories have been publicly published. The case must take place between the publication of *The Sign of the Four* and "Silver Blaze" itself (February 1890 and June 1892).

1890 may be discounted because it can only contain the three cases, as described in "The Final Problem"; "I find that in the year 1890 there were only three cases of which I retain any record." (As previously noted, those three cases are "The Red-Headed League," "The Blue Carbuncle," and "A Case of Identity.") 1892 may be eliminated due to The Great Hiatus. The year must be 1891.

To find a day and month requires a bit more cunning, but is possible because when they arrive it is before dark: "I should like to take a little walk over the moor before it grows dark," and a short while later the sun was beginning to sink behind the stables of Mapleton. If we can calculate when sunset is, we can discover the day.

They set off from London at about ten in the morning on a Thursday ("this is Thursday morning. Why didn't you go down yesterday?"). When they arrive, they talk for around half an hour before going to explore the moor as the sun is setting. If we know how long the train journey took, we can add the times together to get the time of sunset. Helpfully, Holmes tells us the speed of the train: "Our rate at present is fifty-three and a half miles an hour… the telegraph posts upon this line are sixty yards apart, and the calculation is a simple one." Today, UK trains travel at an average speed of sixty-five miles per hour, which is eleven and a half percent faster. This trip now takes seven and a half hours. Increasing that by eleven and a half percent makes it a trip of eight hours and twenty-two minutes for Holmes and Watson. Putting all these figures together means we are looking for a Thursday when the sunset on Dartmoor was around 6:52 pm. This gives us the date of 02 April 1891 when the sunset was 6:51 pm.

Incidentally, Holmes's reluctance to go to King's Pyland on the Tuesday when he was first summoned may be explained by the fact that in "The Final Problem" we are told on 31 March 1891 Holmes "absolutely hampered" the plans of Professor James Moriarty and was, therefore, otherwise engaged.

The Adventure of the Cardboard Box (*CARD*)

First publicly published: January 1893

Main action: August 1889

As *The Sign of the Four* is referenced by Holmes (see below) in this story, we know it can have taken place no earlier than July 1888. Due to the publication date we know it cannot have happened any later than The Great Hiatus.

1890 may be dismissed as "The Final Problem" tells us it should only contain three cases and they are already allocated (see the explanation in my discussion of "Silver Blaze").

Combined with the early remark "It was a blazing hot day in August," we are left with only two possibilities: August 1888 and August 1889.

Near the end of this story, Holmes reveals Watson has already chronicled two adventures "under the names of *A Study in Scarlet* and of *The Sign of Four*." The difficulty is *The Sign of the Four* was not published publicly until February 1890.

The only explanation for this is Watson privately published accounts of his stories before they were publicly published. Watson would have been hard pushed to find time to write and publish an account of *The Sign of the Four* before August 1888, so we are left with this case taking place in August 1889. Unfortunately, I am unable to identify the actual day of the adventure.

The Adventure of the Yellow Face (*YELL*)

First publicly published: February 1893

Main action: April 1884

Watson conveniently indicates the month in his description of a walk he took with Holmes: "the first faint shoots of green were breaking out upon the elms, and the sticky spear-heads of the chestnuts were just beginning to burst into their five-fold leaves." These events naturally occur early in April. The difficulty is in deciding which April.

We can start by limiting the case to being between their meeting in 1881 and the publication date of 1893. The Great Hiatus allows us to exclude 1892 and 1893.

The following years may be dismissed, as Holmes was too busy on other cases: 1883—"The Speckled Band," 1887—"The Reigate Squires," 1890—"Silver Blaze," and 1891—"The Final Problem."

Watson is clearly unmarried and living at 221b in this case, so 1889 may also be eliminated, as he is married in April of that year.

Further limitation may be found from Watson's comment that at this time "Save for the occasional use of cocaine, [Holmes] had no vices." In *A Study in Scarlet*, Watson is unaware of Holmes's drug habit, so 1881 may be eliminated and 1882 is unlikely for the same reason. By 1888 and *The Sign of the Four*, his drug taking was so bad Watson had witnessed him injecting himself "three times a day for many months." Hardly occasional. 1888 may be discounted.

This leaves 1884, 1885, and 1886.

The most likely year is 1884, far enough before the worrying habits of 1888 for his drug taking to still be considered "occasional" but late enough in their relationship for the habit to have fully formed and come to Watson's attention.

This can be confirmed by Holmes's comment that he "was badly in need of a case": he had had no other cases since "The Beryl Coronet" on 10 February 1884.

The Adventure of the Stock-Broker's Clerk (*STOC*)

First publicly published: March 1893

Main action: 01 June 1889

The story starts with Holmes visiting Watson and enquiring after Mary Watson (née Morstan): "I trust that Mrs. Watson has entirely recovered from all the little excitements connected with our adventure of the *Sign of Four*." So it is after the events of July 1888. But Watson has already told us it is "shortly after my marriage," so it cannot be too far beyond it.

When we are also told it is "one morning in June" the matter is settled, and we must be talking about June 1889.

The weekday is given to us when Hall Pycroft tells how he "hammered away until Friday—that is, yesterday." The day was a Saturday, then.

During his chat with Watson, Holmes speaks of the month as "so wet a June as this," which is a great help to finding the day. The Meteorological Office monthly reports tell us June 1889 was a very dry month, in fact. May, however, was exceptionally wet. The only Saturday in June when it would make sense for Holmes to call it wet would be 01 June 1889, when he had no expectations of improvement in the weather.

The Adventure of the *Gloria Scott* (*GLOR*)

First publicly published: April 1893

Main action: Summer 1875

I will make no attempt to place the date when Holmes related the stories of "The *Gloria Scott*" or "The Musgrave Ritual" to Watson. There is not enough evidence. From their conversation in "The Musgrave Ritual," we know "The *Gloria Scott*" was told some time before "The Musgrave Ritual." We also know they are sharing rooms, so it is likely sometime between 1881 and 1889, beyond that we can say no more.

Trevor Senior's voyage on the *Gloria Scott* (back when he was called James Armitage) is clearly stated as having happened in October 1855.

Holmes's involvement in the story takes place during the long vacation while he is at university, so we know it is summer. The year can be deduced by Trevor Senior's comment "For more than twenty years we have led peaceful and useful lives, and we hoped that our past was forever buried." Making it a simple matter of adding twenty to 1855—summer 1875.

Technically of course, if it is *more than* twenty years later, it should be, at earliest, summer 1876, but this does not quite make sense with Holmes's age. If Holmes is in a "break," he intends to return to university for another year at least. He is already twenty-one and it is safe to assume he has completed the usual three years by this age. But he cannot remain at university much longer if the dates of "The Musgrave Ritual" are to make sense. Besides, Trevor Senior has already proved himself unreliable in reporting dates; at one point he claimed the events took place thirty years ago instead of twenty.

The Adventure of the Musgrave Ritual
(*MUSG*)

First publicly published: May 1893

Main action: June 1877

(Regarding the date Holmes told this story to Watson; see my entry for "The *Gloria Scott*.")

The month is easy to discover, as the ritual would not be usable in any other month than June. The ritual itself makes this clear when it says "What was the month? The sixth from the first."

The year takes more consideration. As I have argued in my entry for "The *Gloria Scott*," after his adventures with the Trevor family, Holmes spent one more year at university, leaving in 1876. He tells us that in his first days in London he had very few cases, suggesting a decent period of time passes before Musgrave consults him. The following year seems likely then, making it June 1877.

It may be noted Holmes claims not to have seen Musgrave for four years before this case, in which case the year would be 1880. Quite so, if they enrolled in the same year, but this is by no means necessary. Musgrave may well have been older and left the university in June 1873, just a year after Holmes joined.

The Adventure of the Reigate Squire (*REIG*)

First publicly published: June 1893

Main action: 25 April 1887 to 26 April 1887

Watson tells us "It was some time before the health of my friend Mr. Sherlock Holmes recovered from the strain caused by his immense exertions in the spring of '87," and "On referring to my notes I see that it was upon the 14th of April that I received a telegram from Lyons which informed me that Holmes was lying ill in the Hotel Dulong," giving us the date 14 April 1887 as a starting point.

This is followed up with "Within twenty-four hours I was in his sick-room…," "Three days later we were back in Baker Street," and finally "a week after our return from Lyons we were under the Colonel's roof." The calculation is a simple one; the date of their arrival at the Colonel's is evidently 25 April 1887. All other dates in this story then follow easily.

The Adventure of the Crooked Man (*CROO*)

First publicly published: July 1893

Main action: 16 August 1887 to 17 August 1887

The year for this story can be found in the history of Henry Wood, who was betrayed by James Barclay in the Indian Mutiny. There are a couple of references to it being thirty years since the 1857 mutiny. Nancy Barclay says "I thought you had been dead this thirty years, Henry." And Holmes winds up the case with "You have at least the satisfaction of knowing that for thirty years of his life his conscience bitterly reproached him for this wicked deed…" So the year of Holmes's involvement is 1887.

We also know we are looking for a summer month as we are told Watson becomes involved "one summer night, a few months after [his] marriage." Looking at his marital status for 1887, we find Watson had recently married at the time of "The Naval Treaty" in July but by the time of "The Five Orange Pips" in September his wife had gone to stay with her mother. (Incidentally, this marks the imminent collapse of the marriage.) August seems the only summer option.

We know James Barclay died on a Monday evening soon after Nancy Barclay returned from a short meeting of the Aldershot branch of The Guild of St. George. The date can be deduced when we find in *The Hampshire Advertiser* of Wednesday 24 August 1887 the following news: "On Saturday [20 August], by the invitation of the Rev. Canon Durst, each branch of St. George's Guild went to Winchester." Such a big meeting of all the branches of Hampshire would likely be preceded by smaller meetings of each local branch to make the necessary arrangements. This was the reason Nancy Barclay attended a brief meeting that night. The Monday we seek is 15 August 1887, with all the other dates slotting neatly into place around it.

The Adventure of the Resident Patient (*RESI*)

First publicly published: August 1893

Main action: October 1881

The date of this case is admittedly uncertain as Watson tells us "I cannot be sure of the exact date, for some of my memoranda upon the matter have been mislaid, but it must have been towards the end of the first year during which Holmes and I shared chambers in Baker Street." 1881 is certain, at least.

He also tells us that "It had been a close, rainy day in October." So we now know it was October 1881. Unfortunately, that is as close as we can get; checking weather records does not help to narrow the day down as most of October that year was wet.

It is worth noting here that Watson makes a point of letting us know when he is uncertain of his facts. He does not fudge or fake—he is always honest with us.

The Adventure of the Greek Interpreter (*GREE*)

First publicly published: September 1893

Main action: July 1888

In dating this case, the only clear guidance we are given is "It was after tea on a summer evening." It is also clear Watson is not married at the time.

In this story Mycroft Holmes and Watson meet for the first time. Mycroft tells Watson "I hear of Sherlock everywhere since you became his chronicler." At least one story must have been published publicly, then. We are thus limited to dates after November 1887 but before The Great Hiatus (during which this story is published).

In order for there to be any point in the timeline when the evidence of "The Dying Detective" can be true, it is necessary for Watson to have married Mary Morstan by the end of July 1888 (as we will see later). We can rule out June, as this is supposed to be one of the many months of stagnation which lead to Holmes's cocaine use at the beginning of *The Sign of the Four*. The only opportunity for this story is in early July 1888, after his engagement but before his marriage to Mary Morstan.

The Adventure of the Naval Treaty (*NAVA*)

First publicly published: October 1893

Main action: 27 July 1887 to 30 July 1887

Watson opens by telling us it is "the July which immediately succeeded my marriage." The question, of course, is which marriage?

It is possible to calculate Watson's year of birth from when he took his degree in medicine from London University in 1878, as related in *A Study in Scarlet*. It is safe to assume that Watson had a normal education, which means we can work backwards to a birth year of 1852. We also know that Percy Phelps was the same age as Watson: "During my school-days I had been intimately associated with a lad named Percy Phelps, who was of much the same age as myself, though he was two classes ahead of me." Combined with the information that Percy Phelps is "nearer forty than thirty," we can tell that it must be a year between 1887 and 1891, when both Watson and Phelps would be between thirty-five and thirty-nine.

July 1891 may be ruled out immediately as being during The Great Hiatus. When they see Percy Phelps, Watson describes "A young man, very pale and worn, was lying upon a sofa near the open window, through which came the rich scent of the garden and the balmy summer air." So, choosing between the remaining four years is made easier by looking at the Meteorological Office weather reports for good weather. The weather of July 1888 is described as "chilly." 1889: "the maxima in all cases low for the time of year." 1890: "showers and local thunderstorms." 1887 is the only option, with the best weather notably in the period from the twenty-second to the twenty-ninth.

Thankfully, in his description of the night of the theft Percy states it was "nearly ten weeks ago—to be more accurate, on the twenty-third of May…" Ten weeks after the 23rd of May would be 01 August, so we know it is just before this: as late in July as possible.

Combining this need for a late July date with the weather turning on 30 July 1887 and the need for a clear night when Holmes catches Joseph Harrison stepping "out into the moonlight."

Holmes's vigil at the window of Percy's room must have begun on the evening of 29th.

The Adventure of the Final Problem (*FINA*)

First publicly published: December 1893

Main action: 24 April 1891 to 04 May 1891

Watson states clearly that he has not seen Holmes very much "during the winter of [1890] and the early spring of 1891" until Holmes shows up at his "consulting-room upon the evening of April 24th." So the story begins on 24 April 1891.

Following the account up to his statement "It was on the third of May that we reached the little village of Meiringen" and "on the afternoon of the fourth we set off together," it is easy to trace the course of their travels to Holmes's apparent death on 04 May 1891.

The Hound of the Baskervilles (*HOUN*)

First publicly published: August 1901

Main action: 23 September 1889 to 19 October 1889

The year of this case can be figured out from James Mortimer's stick. It has the date 1884 engraved on it, of which Holmes says it was clearly a leaving present from Charing Cross Hospital and "he left five years ago—the date is on the stick." The year of the story is 1889.

The date of Sir Charles Baskerville's death is given by the papers as 04 May the same year. The rest of the dates are all easily calculated by working backwards or forwards from Watson's reports, which are all conveniently dated.

For such a long, complicated case, it is remarkably easy to date. But then singularity is almost invariably a clue. The more featureless and commonplace a crime is, the more difficult it is to date.

The Adventure of the Empty House (*EMPT*)

First publicly published: September 1903

Main action: 01 April 1894 to 02 April 1894

The murder of Ronald Adair is reported as having occurred "between the hours of ten and eleven-twenty on the night of March 30, 1894." Holmes has been waiting in Montpelier for the opportunity to catch Colonel Sebastian Moran. News of this murder would have been wired to him by Mycroft as soon as he realised the Colonel was involved. Holmes tells Watson "I was about to return when my movements were hastened by the news of this very remarkable Park Lane Mystery," which would have been on 31 March 1894. He would have arrived in London on 01 April 1894 and immediately set about his investigations.

The date Watson and Holmes reunite, then, would be 01 April 1894, with the arrest of Colonel Sebastian Moran taking place in the small hours of the following morning.

In this adventure we are also given an indication as to the movements of Holmes during the Great Hiatus. By Holmes's account, he travelled from the Reichenbach Falls to Florence and almost immediately on to Tibet where he spent two years. From there, in the space of one year, he visited Persia, "looked in" at Mecca, went to Khartoum and then wound up in Montpellier researching tar derivatives and popping over to Grenoble to have a wax bust of himself made and transported to 221b to await his return.

Lots of people have pointed out that this journey seems improbable. I find it difficult to decide. We do know that Holmes often lied to Watson, but usually with good reason. And there is no obvious reason to lie to him here. On the whole, I am inclined to believe this account. However, there is one omission from Holmes's description of his journeys which will be discussed further in my account of "Wisteria Lodge."

Holmes refers at one point to Watson having written up "The Final Problem": "In your picturesque account of the matter, which I read with great interest some months [after 04 May 1891]." This cannot be the publicly published account as it didn't come out until December 1893. My suspicion is Holmes read a copy of an early manuscript Watson penned soon after he returned to London. My-croft, keeping an eye on Watson, had it pilfered, copied and sent on to Holmes.

I note here that when Watson comments "in some manner [Holmes] had learned of my own sad bereavement," the vagueness of "in some manner" becomes less puzzling in light of my conclusions regarding "Wisteria Lodge." As does his decision to transport a wax bust of himself to 221b when, we are led to believe, Mrs. Hudson thought him dead.

The Adventure of the Norwood Builder
(*NORW*)

First publicly published: October 1903

Main action: 11 August 1894 to 12 August 1894

The year and month are easily found in the story. "At the time of which I speak Holmes had been back [from hiatus] for some months," so it is still 1894. And later Holmes says he "crawled about the lawn with an August sun on my back." So August 1894 seems fairly obvious.

In the Meteorological Office monthly reports for that month, we discover "August was exceedingly cloudy and unsettled, with frequent thunderstorms and with heavy falls of rain." For most of the month Holmes would have had a hard job crawling about with the sun on his back. It was only on the 10th and 11th that there was a brief improvement in the weather. If Jonas Oldacre got a fire going in his yard on the first clear day, this leaves the second for Holmes's sunny day investigation when he was first brought in on the case.

The Adventure of the Dancing Men (*DANC*)

First publicly published: December 1903

Main action: 27 July 1898 to 13 August 1898

The key to establishing the date of this case is in Hilton Cubitt's original talk with Holmes: "Last year I came up to London for the Jubilee." The case takes place in the year after the jubilee celebrations. Easy. Until you look up Queen Victoria's jubilee celebrations and see she had two: the Golden Jubilee in June 1887 and the Diamond Jubilee in 1897.

The decision can only be made by researching the jubilees themselves. The Diamond Jubilee was a much bigger affair and far more likely to have attracted someone all the way from Norfolk, such as Hilton. This is supported by Watson being seemingly unmarried and living at 221b in "The Dancing Men," which makes 1898 a far more suitable year than 1888.

Cubitt's further statement that he had "been married now for a year" places this case in or after June 1898. This is confirmed by him telling us the first troubles came in his marriage "about a month ago, at the end of June." We are at the end of July at the time he comes to Holmes.

As I was only able to deduce the year and month on my own, I turned to William S. Baring-Gould's *Annotated Sherlock Holmes* for help. In Volume II, page 530, note 7, there is an interesting observation about Watson's billiards game.

Remember that Hilton said it was "About a week ago—it was the Tuesday of last week" during the initial consultation. That "About" means that the day of the consultation is not itself a Tuesday but one of the days either side of it; Monday or Wednesday. In their conversation at the start of the story Holmes reveals that Watson had spent the previous evening playing billiards at his club with Thurston. If the consultation is on a Monday or Wednesday, the billiards evening must be either Sunday or Tuesday. As he unlikely to have been playing billiards at his club on a Sunday, it must have been the Tuesday. So the consultation was on a Wednesday. It is a short step to finding the Wednesday in question would be 27 July 1898.

The Adventure of the Solitary Cyclist (*SOLI*)

First publicly published: December 1903

Main action: 27 April 1895 to 04 May 1895

The date of this case is given in Watson's introduction: "On referring to my note-book for the year 1895 I find that it was upon Saturday, the 23rd of April, that we first heard of Miss Violet Smith."

Unfortunately, I am forced by this narrative to turn hypocrite. I must temporarily recant one of my own premises. 23 April 1895 was a Tuesday, not a Saturday. It is with great reluctance that I must accuse Watson of misreading his own notes. Just this once. Only once.

The facts of the story make it clear the initial consultation did take place on a Saturday. This is the day of the week when Violet Smith cycled to the train station and came into town. But Watson is so certain about the date he gives that somehow it must also be true.

The only explanation I have to offer is as follows. This story was published in the middle of one of Watson's prolific writing periods (that which is collected under the title *The Return of Sherlock Holmes*). In his haste to put the stories together for *The Strand*'s deadlines, he erred when reading his notes and compounded two dates. Tuesday 23 April 1895 is when they first heard of Violet Smith. It is when a letter arrived informing them of her intention to visit. Saturday 27 April 1895 is when Violet Smith arrived at 221b for her consultation with Holmes. Thus we may emerge with Watson's integrity (just about) intact.

The Adventure of the Priory School (*PRIO*)

First publicly published: January 1904

Main action: 16 May 1901 to 18 May 1901

This case is quickly limited to when it could take place when Holmes looks up the Duke of Holdernesse and finds it recorded that he has been "Lord Lieutenant of Hallamshire since 1900." It must be between 1900 and 1904, when this story is published.

We are given a further clue when, in describing Lord Saltire's abduction, Dr. Thorneycroft Huxtable says "He was last seen on the night of May 13th—that is, the night of last Monday." Only one year in our range has a Monday 13 May, and that is 1901.

The Adventure of Black Peter (*BLAC*)

First publicly published: February 1904

Main action: 10 July 1895 to 12 July 1895

This case is fairly clearly dated by Watson in his introduction: "I have never known my friend to be in better form, both mental and physical, than in the year '95." We are told that the case begins for Holmes "during the first week of July."

While filling in Watson on the details of Peter Carey's murder, Holmes tells us that "he died just a week ago to-day," and that "the crime was done upon the Wednesday." This conversation takes place just after "the first week of July," so we can conclude the Wednesday he confides in Watson is 10 July 1895.

It may be pointed out that 10 July is not during "the first week of July." However, by "the first week of July" Watson meant 03 July to 10 July 1895: the first whole week to fall within July. This is not the first seven days of July, but we needn't assume that's what Watson meant.

Note—there is a reference in this story to "The Priory School," which may confuse the unwary: "save in the case of the Duke of Holdernesse, I have seldom known him claim any large reward for his inestimable services." This reference may lead one to assume "Black Peter" took place after "The Priory School." I date "Black Peter" in 1895 and "Priory School" in 1901. Watson referenced the 1901 "Priory School" in his text for the 1895 "Black Peter" because he didn't write the 1895 tale until near its 1904 publication date.

The Adventure of Charles Augustus Milverton (*CHAS*)

First publicly published: March 1904

Main action: 04 January 1886 to 14 January 1886

Watson tells us at the beginning of this story that he intends to "conceal the date or any other fact by which [the reader] might trace the actual occurrence." We might expect this to be a difficult one to pin down.

There are some clues, though. Watson states that the adventure comes to his attention "about six o'clock on a cold, frosty winter's evening." (We can trust that it really is winter as the fire blazing in Charles Augustus Milverton's office later on is integral to the plot.) It must be a winter month; December, January, or February.

Chatting about their intention to burgle Milverton, Holmes remarks that "We have shared the same room for some years, and it would be amusing if we ended by sharing the same cell." This suggests two things. First, they have already been living together for more than a few years; it is at earliest January 1884. Secondly, that they have yet to be separated by one of Watson's marriages; it is no later than January 1887.

There is also a chat with Milverton himself in which he assures Holmes "if the money is not paid on the 14th there certainly will be no marriage on the 18th."

When they arrive at Milverton's office they find the fire lit and doors still open. Holmes had gone to great lengths to ensure there would be no one up when they broke in. We would expect that, finding his plans disrupted, he would abandon the attempt and try again another night. Instead he whispers to Watson "I don't like it… I can't quite make it out. Anyhow, we have no time to lose." Why is there no time to lose? Why can they not leave and try again tomorrow? The only explanation is that another night would be too late: the evening of the break in is the day before the deadline. It is the night of the 13th.

The night that they burgle Milverton suits Holmes's purposes as it is "a wild, tempestuous evening, when the wind screamed and rattled against the windows" that should help to conceal them. Again, being integral to events, we may trust this information.

A trawl through Meteorological Office records reveals that there is only one winter 13th between 1884 and 1887 that meets these requirements: 13 January 1886. The *London Daily News* of 14 January 1886 confirms this, reporting the wind blowing "very strongly from north-west during the latter part of the day" and much higher rainfall than the previous two days.

The Adventure of the Six Napoleons (*SIXN*)

First publicly published: April 1904

Main action: June 1900

The night of Beppo's arrest is sometime after his last pay day and the records of Gelder and Co. tell us "he was paid last on May 20th." As Victorian pay day would usually have been a Saturday, we can immediately whittle our search down to a Saturday 20 May.

Towards the end of the case, Holmes says to Watson "If ever I permit you to chronicle any more of my little problems, Watson, I foresee that you will enliven your pages by an account of the singular adventure of the Napoleonic busts," heavily suggesting that this case took place during a period when Watson was not regularly publishing his accounts. The obvious period is the gap from 1894 to 1903. Pay day would be one year (the length of Beppo's jail term) earlier—sometime between 1893 and 1902.

During these years there are only two occurrences of Saturday 20 May, in 1893 and 1899, which would put Holmes's involvement a year later, in either 1894 or 1900.

The case comes to Holmes during a social visit from Lestrade. These seem to be a regular occurrence at the time and represent a change in the relationship between the official and unofficial detectives. Certainly such a visit would not have taken place in the early days of *A Study in Scarlet*. Looking at the attitude of Lestrade in an 1894 case, "The Norwood Builder," we can see the beginning of a change, but the tension between them still rules out such visits taking place. The year of these social visits must be 1900.

Beppo would have been paid weekly so he must have been caught within a week of his last payday (20 May 1899). Then he would have had to wait a short while for his trial, at which point he was sentenced to a year in jail. He would have got out either at the end of May or early in June 1900. Shortly after his release he would have started the detective work needed to find the batch of Napoleons which hid the pearl. Therefore, the busts being smashed and Holmes becoming involved would have taken place in June 1900.

The Adventure of the Three Students (*3STU*)

First publicly published: June 1904

Main action: 15 March 1895 to 16 March 1895

The year for the case is given as 1895 and it only remains for us to establish the day and month.

I should state here that my dating of this case relies heavily on Nick Utechin's work proving that Holmes attended St. John's College, Oxford. The issue of Holmes being an Oxford boy has always seemed obvious to me, given his opinions of Cambridge in "The Missing Three-Quarter." The point has certainly been proved to my satisfaction and if you are in any doubt yourself, you could do worse than consulting *Sherlock Holmes at Oxford* by Nicholas Utechin.

We are also told that Hilton Soames, the client of this case, is an acquaintance of Holmes and Watson. It seems clear this is because he was once Holmes's lecturer, in which case Soames must also come from St. John's College.

Our clue to the date lies in the statement that Soames found his test disturbed at 5:30 pm. He then briefly spoke with Bannister and set off to get Holmes from his rooms by the library. They conversed and then went back to Soames's office. At which point Watson reports "It was already twilight."

With Hilton Soames on the grounds of St. John's College and Holmes in a room near the Bodleian Library, it easy to calculate how long the walk took using Google Maps: nine minutes each way. Watson records the conversation that took place in their room verbatim. I re-enacted the discussion and timed it, this also took nine minutes (give or take a few seconds). Add up all these times and we find we are looking for a day when it would have been twilight at 5:57 pm.

The date we come up with is 15 March 1895, when the sunset in Oxford was at 6:09 pm.

The Adventure of the Golden Pince-Nez (*GOLD*)

First publicly published: July 1904

Main action: 15 November 1894 to 16 November 1894

Watson kicks this story off by telling us it took place in 1894 and "it was a wild, tempestuous night towards the close of November," but "the gale had blown itself out next day."

All that remains is to check the Meteorological Office records for the last half of November 1894 for some particularly bad weather.

The question is settled by the following: "a tremendous downpour occurred between 11th and 14th. After the 15th, however, a gradual improvement set in..." The last of the stormy weather on 15 November 1894 is what Watson refers to, and its having blown itself out happens the following day.

The Adventure of the Missing Three-Quarter (*MISS*)

First publicly published: August 1904

Main action: 13 December 1897 to 15 December 1897

The year of this case is limited by Watson stating it is "some seven or eight years ago." With the story being one of thirteen written to deadline for the *Return of Sherlock Holmes* batch of stories, we can assume it was written shortly before the publication date of 1904. That makes the case happen in either 1897 or 1898.

A check of the Varsity Match results shows us it must be 1897, when Oxford won, as in the story.

The Varsity Match was always played on the second Tuesday in December, but Watson says it is "a gloomy February morning." Of course, this is another example of Watson waxing lyrical. February typically brings the worst of winter to England. Watson is simply saying that it was especially grotty weather. Being a rugby player himself, it is likely that Watson assumed the reference to the Varsity Match would make it abundantly clear what the actual date was and so provided no further clarification.

Cyril Overton handily tells us the match is to take place the day after he consults Holmes. That would have been 14 December 1897, putting the consultation on 13 December 1897.

The Adventure of the Abbey Grange (*ABBE*)

First publicly published: September 1904

Main action: 18 January 1897 to 20 January 1897

"It was on a bitterly cold and frosty morning during the winter of '97" when this story gets going. Most of the rest of the dating is based around the regrettable decision of Miss Mary Fraser to marry Sir Eustace Brackenstall.

Mary's maid tells us that "we met [Sir Eustace], only eighteen months ago," when Mary "had only just arrived in London… We arrived in June, and it was July. They were married in January of last year." If they have known each other eighteen months since they met in early July, then the action of the case is taking place in January 1897.

From there we need only look for remarkably bitter weather for a January and we find it once again in the Meteorological Office reports: "Lowest reading occurred… mostly between the 17th and 19th." Making 18 January 1897 the coldest day.

The Adventure of the Second Stain (*SECO*)

First publicly published: December 1904

Main action: Autumn 1886

Watson informs us he has purposely obscured the details of the case: "It was, then, in a year, and even in a decade, that shall be nameless, that upon one Tuesday morning in autumn…"

I admit Watson beat me: I could not figure the date out. Reluctantly, I had to turn to William S. Baring-Gould's *Annotated Sherlock Holmes*, Volume I, page 303, note 7, where he details Gavin Brend's argument regarding the holding of political offices. It is based upon the fact that Lord Bellinger is the prime minister and Trelawney Hope is foreign secretary. I quote:

> "The case must… have occurred in the autumn of a year when the offices of Prime Minister and Foreign Secretary were held by two different men. But only the first year [of Lord Salisbury's second period as Prime Minister], 1886, meets this requirement."

The Adventure of Wisteria Lodge (*WIST*)

First publicly published: August 1908

Main action: 19 March 1892 to 24 March 1892

This case is often considered a problem for chronologists, because Watson clearly states the adventure begins on "a bleak and windy day towards the end of March in the year 1892." 1892—during The Great Hiatus—when Watson believes Holmes to be dead at the bottom of the Reichenbach Falls.

"Impossible!" you cry. "He *must* have the date wrong!"

No. If Watson says it happened in 1892, it happened in 1892; Watson does not lie. But how is this possible?

Recall, if you will, that when Holmes returned in "The Empty House" he had somehow learned of Watson's "sad bereavement." My proposal is this was the death of a wife in 1892. For whatever reason, Watson was more upset than usual when this one died and he began to go off the rails. Brain fever, he would have called it. Watson needed help urgently.

Fortunately for the doctor, Mycroft was keeping an eye on him from afar. Mycroft relayed the news of Watson's ill health to Holmes and between them they arranged a secret return to 221b so that Holmes could help Watson back on his feet. Holmes provided assistance the only way he knew: "Work is the best antidote to sorrow, my dear Watson." They solved two cases together before Holmes returned to The Hiatus: an unpublished one that resulted in the arrest of Colonel Carruthers (mentioned at the start of this adventure) and then "Wisteria Lodge."

There are difficulties, of course. One is the large number of people who would need to be in on this secret. Let us consider each of the people mentioned in this story.

Mycroft is not a problem; we already know from "The Empty House" that he was in on the Hiatus deception.

Mrs. Hudson would have to know about the secret plot for Holmes to be able to return to 221b. But it is likely she already knew. In "The Empty House" we are told she has been keeping his rooms for him for the duration of his "death." The explanation Holmes gives to Watson is that Mycroft had been paying her and telling her he wanted the rooms kept as a sort of shrine. Mrs. Hudson isn't stupid enough to believe such a silly request from unsentimental Mycroft. I believe she was always in on Holmes's secret survival. The only reason Holmes claims she wasn't is to avoid upsetting Watson. Note that Watson is not there for the moment Holmes reveals his resurrection to Hudson in "The Empty House"; he is just told about it by Holmes.

What of the other characters in this story, then? Actually, there are not so very many to worry about. As members of the police force, Inspectors Gregson and Baynes and Constable Walters could be sworn to secrecy. (The right word from Mycroft to the right police chiefs might further aid them in keeping silent.) There is also Miss Burnett, who is rescued from Don Juan Murillo's clutches. But, if she is capable of playing the double agent in an enemy's house for so long, her promise to keep this secret could be trusted. If necessary, it would be easy to get such a promise by holding a charge of conspiracy or similar over her. As for the boy working for Mrs. Hudson at 221b, he was one of the loyal irregulars and we can certainly trust them.

Scott Eccles is a different sort of anomaly. Why would he contact Holmes with his problem if he believed Holmes to be dead? The question is based on a false assumption. He didn't know Holmes was dead. We learn in "The Final Problem" how limited the reports had been of Holmes's death. By 1892 there had only been a couple of brief notices in the papers the previous year. He could easily have missed these. The vitriolic letters of Moriarty's brother that caused Watson to write his famous account would not be published for another year. Once his case was solved, no doubt Eccles would have gratefully agreed to keep Holmes's secret for a few years.

The only genuine difficulty is Watson himself. Why was he not shocked when Holmes returned in 1892? And why did he appear to think Holmes was dead when he wrote "The Final Problem" a year later? I'll wager Holmes and Mycroft used a hypnotist. Watson was hypnotised just before Holmes's return to make him think living at 221b with Holmes was still the norm. He woke in his old room and the charade began. When it was time for Holmes to leave him again, Watson was hypnotised to forget the entire return. This had to be done so that he could not inadvertently expose Holmes in his actions or writings—remember that Watson is a useless liar and Holmes could not trust such an important secret to him. But the subconscious healing was done, and Watson was left more able to cope until Holmes's permanent resurrection two years later.

This explains why Holmes was so surprised on his second return in April 1894 when Watson fainted: "I owe you a thousand apologies. I had no idea that you would be so affected." After all, he never got that reaction in 1892!

It may be tempting for chronologists to use this excuse to place many other cases in 1892. This would be a mistake. If there were more cases, too many other people would need to be sworn to secrecy. That's not a risk either of the Holmes brothers would have been willing to take.

The actual day of the month, incidentally, is discovered when Scott Eccles says that "quarter-day is at hand," which would be 25 March 1892. We can be sure that his visit to Wisteria Lodge would have taken place on a weekend, therefore it took place on the weekend before 25 March 1892.

The Adventure of the Bruce-Partington Plans
(*BRUC*)

First publicly published: December 1908

Main action: 22 November 1895 to 23 November 1895

This is a very simple case to date as Watson starts by telling us about "the third week of November, in the year 1895...." There follow details of how they spent several days culminating in a visit from Mycroft on Thursday. That would have to be Thursday 21 November 1895.

There are no difficulties in placing the events in their proper places once we have established this as our start.

The Adventure of the Devil's Foot (*DEVI*)

First publicly published: December 1910

Main action: 16 March 1897 to 18 March 1897

The date for this adventure is scattered among the opening few paragraphs. "In the spring of the year 1897" … "in March of that year" Dr. Agar convinces Holmes to take a holiday.

Shortly afterwards the vicar and the villain show up at their holiday cottage "on Tuesday, March the 16th." This is the start of the case and gives us the point from which all other dates surrounding the events of Poldhu Bay may be calculated.

The Adventure of the Red Circle (*REDC*)

First publicly published: March 1911

Main action: 24 September 1902 to 25 September 1902

The main clue to the date of this case is when Holmes remarks upon a corner of paper which has been torn off because "there was evidently some mark, some thumbprint, something which might give a clue to the person's identity." This comment would only make sense after July 1901, when the Metropolitan Police first began using fingerprints to identify people. The case must take place sometime between 1901 and Holmes's retirement by 1904.

With this limitation in mind, the case can be further dated by its last lines: "By the way, it is not eight o'clock, and a Wagner night at Covent Garden! If we hurry, we might be in time for the second act."

If you search the British Newspaper Archive for "Covent Garden" and "Wagner," it does not take very long to come across the *Daily Telegraph & Courier* (and several other papers) on 26 September 1902 reporting on the success of the Wagner evening at Covent Garden the night before.

This is the only concert I could find that would account for Holmes's remark, and so we can work backwards from it to date the whole case.

The Disappearance of Lady Frances Carfax
(*LADY*)

First publicly published: December 1911

Main action: Autumn 1894

Lady Frances Carfax's would-be suitor in this case is Philip Green who has made his money in the gold fields of Barberton, South Africa. A little research into the Barberton Gold Rush turned up an article in the *South Wales Daily Post* of 13 December 1895, which tells that "renewed" attention was being given to the area. This suggests that the gold rush proper had already petered out. The latest Philip would have left with a fortune must be 1894.

We can combine this information with the description of Holy Peters who "was badly bitten in a saloon-fight at Adelaide in '89" to limit our search to the years from 1891 to 1894. (In 1889 the fight would have been reported as "this year" and in 1890 it would be "last year.")

1892 and 1893 can be eliminated as being during The Great Hiatus.

If we consider that Lady Carfax was likely to be in Europe for what was known as The Continental Season, we can follow the events and see that she was most likely abducted in the autumn. Autumn 1891 was also during The Great Hiatus.

We are left, through process of elimination, with a case taking place in autumn 1894.

The Adventure of the Dying Detective (*DYIN*)

First publicly published: November 1913

Main action: 03 August 1889

The dating of this case hinges on Watson's marriages. He tells us Mrs. Hudson "came to my rooms in the second year of my married life and told me of the sad condition to which my poor friend was reduced."

It is difficult to find one of Watson's marriages which made it to its second year. For sure, there is only one during the active years with Holmes: his marriage to Mary Morstan which lasted from late July 1888 all the way through to late August 1889.

Confusingly, the only reason we know the length of this marriage is because we know from "The Dying Detective" that Watson has a marriage that lasts into its second year and the only one that can be made to fit is the one to Mary Morstan. All other Watson marriages are demonstrably over within a year or take place after Holmes's retirement. He proposes to Mary in June 1888 but is not married during "The Greek Interpreter" in early July 1888. By the time of "The Cardboard Box" in August 1889, he is no longer married. The marriage must (due to the necessity of a marriage over one year) be pinned from late July (just after "The Greek Interpreter") to sometime in August (just before "The Cardboard Box").

This only gives us August 1889 in which Watson can claim to be in the second year of a marriage.

The only other difficulty is that Watson uses a poetic "In the dim light of a foggy November day the sick room was a gloomy spot" to describe the day. Once again, he is not being literal. He is making the point that this August day was appalling, weather-wise. We must seek a day when the weather was especially bad. A quick look at the Meteorological Office report published in the *London Evening Standard* for 03 August 1889 shows that it was a day of strong winds, south-westerly gales and rain. That is our day, then.

The Valley of Fear (*VALL*)

First publicly published: September 1914

Main Holmes action: 07 January 1887 to 08 January 1887

Vermissa Valley action: 04 February 1867 to 15 May 1867

Holmes's involvement in this case took place during "the early days at the end of the '80's," which limits us to between 1886 and 1889. We also know that "being the seventh of January, [they] have very properly laid in the new almanac."

From the details of the story we can tell that Watson is unmarried and living at 221b. In January 1888 and 1889 Watson is married. So these years are ruled out.

In January 1886 Holmes was busy courting Charles Augustus Milverton's maid in the guise of Escott the plumber.

So, by process of elimination we know that the case starts with the attempt to break Porlock's code on 07 January 1887.

This does leave us with the difficulty of Watson and Holmes discussing Moriarty in 1887 and then Watson claiming never to have heard of Moriarty in 1891 during "The Final Problem." I can see two explanations and I invite you to take your pick.

Option one: Watson is using a literary device in "The Final Problem." When telling us that story, he needed to introduce us to the character for the first time. The first conversation he ever had with Holmes about Moriarty would perform this function nicely. To make it easy on himself, he transposed a conversation from before *The Valley of Fear* into "The Final Problem." I don't like this explanation as it involves Watson lying to us. Not much of a lie, but still more of a lie than I like to accept.

Option two: Watson knew about Moriarty early on. However, as Holmes's investigations went deeper, he realised the danger he put Watson in by disclosing any information to him. Worse, Holmes could not stay hidden from the Napoleon of Crime if Watson accidentally mentioned Moriarty in one of his published accounts. As he would do again later in "Wisteria Lodge," Holmes was forced to bring in a hypnotist to wipe Moriarty from Watson's mind. The recorded conversation in "The Final Problem" remains a truthful account. Improbable though it may seem, this is preferable to an impossibly deceitful Watson.

The Vermissa Valley story related from John Douglas's manuscript should also be a straightforward one to date. It starts: "It was the fourth of February in the year 1875," and we can certainly figure out many of the dates from there.

But Watson introduces the case by inviting us "to journey back some twenty years in time," no doubt because Douglas told him at some point that it happened twenty years ago. This should take us back to 1867, not 1875.

We see a similar problem when, as part of his account, John Douglas writes things had never been as hopeless "as in the early summer." But the period he is referring to should be spring if we follow the passage of time in his tale correctly.

However, we must consider what Watson is working with here. While cramped in his hiding place, John Douglas had been scribbling his notes in near darkness. In his own words: "I've been cooped up two days, and I've spent the daylight hours—as much daylight as I could get in that rat trap—in putting the thing into words."

Is it any wonder that Watson had trouble reading the notes? He was bound to make mistakes reading such a poorly composed manuscript. By the time he was done writing it up, Douglas had fled the country and soon after was murdered. It's not like he could get Douglas to check the facts for his part of the story. To be sure, it is not that Watson has lied; he has misread someone else's scrawls and reported them in a manner he took to be accurate. Nevertheless, it is necessary to correct Watson's misreading when dating the Douglas story. It is difficult to make sense of the years Douglas spent after Vermissa Valley if we take the 1875 start as correct. Therefore, it must start on 04 February 1867.

His Last Bow (*LAST*)

First publicly published: September 1917

Main action: 02 August 1914 to 03 August 1914

"It was nine o'clock at night upon the second of August—the most terrible August in the history of the world."

This is 02 August 1914, the day before England was drawn in to the First World War. All chronologists agree that this one date is unquestionably correct.

The Adventure of the Mazarin Stone (*MAZA*)

First publicly published: October 1921

Main action: Summer 1903

This is one of those stories in which Watson was not present for all the events and is working from other people's accounts and some guesswork. He indicates this by writing in the third person. (See also "His Last Bow," the second part of *A Study in Scarlet* and part two of *The Valley of Fear*.)

All we have to indicate a date in the text is "It was seven in the evening of a lovely summer's day." We are looking for a summer month.

The main clue to the year is Holmes's use of the Gramophone. He says: "These modern gramophones are a remarkable invention." The Gramophone Company was founded in 1898, so the case must have taken place after that and before Holmes's retirement. (Technically, as a brand name, the Gramophone in Holmes's statement should be capitalised, but when Watson wrote the case up in 1921 the name had become synonymous with any brand of phonograph, so the mistake is forgivable.)

We are told that "It was pleasant to Dr. Watson to find himself once more in the untidy room of the first floor in Baker Street which had been the starting-point of so many remarkable adventures." Indicating a summer when Watson is not at 221b and has not been for a little while. This rules out 1898 through 1901. Summer 1902 also seems to be a period when Watson is at 221b, although he has moved into rooms in Queen Anne Street by September. Holmes is most likely already in his retirement cottage by summer 1904, so that won't do either.

In light of Holmes's remark in January 1903 that Watson had "deserted" him (see "The Blanched Soldier"), the summer of that same year would account for the joy Watson finds in an unexpected return to 221b.

The Problem of Thor Bridge (*THOR*)

First publicly published: February 1922

Main action: 04 October 1900 to 06 October 1900

The month of this case is stated clearly at the start: "It was a wild morning in October." The day may be found later on when Holmes shows Watson a letter he received the previous day from Claridge's Hotel, which is dated "October 3rd."

Unfortunately, none of these clues narrow things down enough. Unhappily, I had to turn to William S. Baring-Gould's excellent *Annotated Sherlock Holmes* for help. There I found in Volume II, page 590, note 9, H.W. Bell's brilliant discovery regarding the *Family Herald*. We are told that the breakfast eggs are not their best, because the cook got in the *Family Herald* the day before. The *Family Herald* was published on Wednesdays. Therefore, the day the case starts is a Thursday 04 October. We are now limited to four possible years: 1883, 1888, 1894, and 1900.

Returning to Watson's statement that "It was a wild morning," we can check the Meteorological Office reports to narrow down the options. The weather in October 1883 was fair, '88 had light winds, '94 was varied, but 1900 has the following entry: "Gales were rather frequent during the earlier half of the month."

The start date is found, then: 04 October 1900.

The Adventure of the Creeping Man (*CREE*)

First publicly published: March 1923

Main action: 06 September 1903 to 15 September 1903

Watson is summoned to this case by Holmes "one Sunday evening early in September of the year 1903." That limits it to the first two Sundays of September 1903, either the sixth or the thirteenth. With the thirteenth being more like mid-September than early September, the date this case gets going is 06 September 1903.

We are also told during this case that Holmes has started using a general utility man named Mercer since Watson last lived with him. As far as I can tell, this would be around September 1902. However, I am too uncertain of a date to be willing to put the start of Mercer's employment on my timeline.

The Adventure of the Sussex Vampire (*SUSS*)

First publicly published: January 1924

Main action: 20 November 1897

A letter from Morrison, Morrison, and Dodd dated 19 November starts this story, leaving just the year to find.

Checking his index books, Holmes remarks "Voyage of the *Gloria Scott*, … That was a bad business. I have some recollection that you made a record of it." So, this adventure takes place after the publication of "The *Gloria Scott*" in April 1893 and the use of "some recollection" suggests several years have passed.

Luckily there is a distinct weather pattern to look for, because Watson relates "it was evening of a dull, foggy November day" when they travelled to the Ferguson household in Sussex.

Ignoring the Great Hiatus, the weather records reveal three years as contenders. 1898 is mentioned as having mist. 1902 has occasional fogs (but also snow, which Watson would surely have mentioned). But 1897 is the most likely, with "a good deal of cloud and fog." The case takes place, then, on 20 November 1897.

The Adventure of the Three Garridebs
(*3GAR*)

First publicly published: October 1924

Main action: 26 June 1902 to 27 June 1902

We are given a good indication of the date by Watson, who tells us that Holmes's refusal of a knighthood "enables me to fix the date, which was the latter end of June, 1902."

Nathan Garrideb provides the information that the American "Garrideb" called on him two days ago—which was "last Tuesday," so we know we are looking for a Thursday in the last half of June 1902. There are only two options: the 19th and the 26th. With the nineteenth being more like the middle of June than "the latter end of June," we arrive at a start date of 26 June 1902.

The Adventure of the Illustrious Client (*ILLU*)

First publicly published: November 1924

Main action: 03 September 1902 to 15 September 1902

This adventure starts with Holmes and Watson in the Turkish baths of Northumberland Avenue in which "there is an isolated corner where two couches lie side by side, and it was on these that we lay upon September 3, 1902, the day when my narrative begins."

If only all of Watson's reports gave the exact date in the second paragraph, we might be saved a good many headaches.

It should be noted that Watson attempts to lie in this story. By posing as a collector of Chinese pottery, he tries to distract Baron Adelbert Gruner. Here we see what an example of what a poor liar Watson is; the Baron is on to Watson's ruse in next to no time.

The Adventure of the Three Gables (*3GAB*)

First publicly published: September 1926

Main action: Summer 1902

After the burglary at the Three Gables, the inspector mentions "the chance of finger-marks or something." Given that the Metropolitan Police did not start using fingerprints until July 1901, the case must take place after this date.

Watson seems to be living at 221b. Looking at his marital status in other adventures, this case must occur before January 1903 ("The Blanched Soldier") and probably before September 1902 ("The Illustrious Client").

I am indebted to H.W. Bell via Gould's *Annotated Sherlock Holmes*, Volume II, Page 729, note 9, for the pointer to the inferences which may be drawn from the mention that "a couple of constables were examining the windows and the geranium beds." It must be May at the earliest for the geraniums to have been planted out. More likely, for the geranium beds to really look like geranium beds, we are in the summer months.

The only reasonable period to place this story is summer 1902.

The Adventure of the Blanched Soldier (*BLAN*)

First publicly published: October 1926

Main action: 21 January 1903 to 26 January 1903

This story is written by Holmes and as such it is perhaps less reliable than others, given Holmes's propensity for untruths. However, we can take comfort in the knowledge that it is Holmes who decided to write the story and therefore, presumably, wishes us to know the truth.

"I find from my notebook that it was in January, 1903," he begins. Leaving just the day to ascertain.

James M. Dodd wants to look up his friend Godfrey Emsworth and he tells Holmes that he made a trip to the family home on the previous Monday and at that time saw his friend's face at the window. We learn later on that Godfrey is seriously ill, making a night-time visit in any poor weather unlikely. The first week of that month was unsettled, with frequent rain and thunderstorms. This rules out the fifth. From the ninth "for nearly a week a frost of considerable severity prevailed," which rules out Monday the twelfth. "Between the 25th and 27th thunder and lightning occurred," ruling out Monday the 26th.

Monday 19 January 1903 is the only possible night for James to have seen Godfrey at the window of his family home. From this date all the rest may be worked out.

The Adventure of the Lion's Mane (*LION*)

First publicly published: November 1926

Main action: 23 July 1907 to 31 July 1907

As with "The Blanched Soldier," we are forced to take Holmes's word on the facts of this case. Nevertheless, we have little reason to doubt his report.

Holmes tells us this adventure takes place "towards the end of July, 1907" when "there was a severe gale" but that "on the morning of which I speak the wind had abated." We are seeking a windy period in Sussex at the end of July 1907.

With this much information, it is not difficult to find the right Meteorological Office report: "Thunderstorms… occurred on twenty-four days [of July 1907]… those of the 21st and 22nd appear to have been of extraordinary violence."

The storms had just about abated on 23 July 1907, which is when this story begins.

The Adventure of the Retired Colourman
(*RETI*)

First publicly published: December 1926

Main action: 04 June 1899 to 06 June 1899

Giving Watson the details of the case, Holmes says Josiah Amberley married in 1897 and within two years is a broken man. The year must be 1899.

Watson is sent off to see Josiah at his home "and so it was that on a summer afternoon [he] set forth to Lewisham," revealing it is summer 1899.

There is only one way to get a more specific date: by identifying who the "Carina" is that Holmes goes to see sing at the Albert Hall on the evening of the first day of the case. Sadly, no such singer seems to exist. Either Watson misheard or Holmes is lying. By accepting the former, some progress may be made.

The Royal Albert Hall website contains a very user-friendly archive. A search through the performances of summer 1899 yields one Sunday Concert which seems much more likely than all the others.

On 04 June 1899, Clarissa Talbot sang. It is conceivable that Watson heard "Carina" when Holmes said "Clarissa." This is made more likely by the set list for the concert. It contains at least two of Holmes's known favourite composers. There is "Hear Ye, Israel" by Mendelssohn and "Der Ritt der Walkuren" by Wagner.

Using this concert as the "Carina" concert, the case may be dated as beginning on 04 June 1899.

The Adventure of the Veiled Lodger (*VEIL*)

First publicly published: January 1927

Main action: Last third of 1896

Original Crime: First half of 1889

The crimes and confessions of Mrs. Ronder are impossible to date very specifically.

We are told the confession part of the story starts "late in 1896," limiting it to the last third of that year.

Holmes then goes on to relate the murder of Mr. Ronder and mauling of Mrs. Ronder took place "seven years ago." Meaning the crime part of the story happened in 1889.

After she was mauled, "it was six months before she was fit to give evidence," after which she went into lodgings with Mrs. Merrilow. Given that Mrs. Merrilow makes it clear that she came as a lodger in 1889, (the same year as she was mauled six months previously) the mauling must have occurred in the first half of the year.

The Adventure of Shoscombe Old Place (*SHOS*)

First publicly published: March 1927

Main action: 05 May 1883 to 06 May 1883

To date this story, all Watson expressly gives us is that "it was… a bright May evening" when they took the train to Shoscombe Old Place.

In a conversation between Holmes and Watson, they suggest Robert Norberton is unlikely to be guilty because he is a Lord:

> "My dear Holmes, it is out of the question."
> "Very possibly, Watson. Sir Robert is a man of an honourable stock."

Given the highly dishonourable conduct of several noblemen in their later adventures, this must be an early case. Certainly, this must be before the unseemly behaviour of a king in "A Scandal in Bohemia." So the date is limited to the years 1881 to 1887 inclusive.

To continue, it is necessary to combine several pieces of information. Firstly, "It was pitch-dark and without a moon" when Holmes, Watson, and Mason examined the family crypt. This is the day after Mason first consults them. Mason first consults them a week after Lady Beatrice stops visiting the horses (that is, a week after she dies). Therefore, there was a moonless night eight days after the death of Lady Beatrice Falder.

Secondly, based on Sir Robert Norberton's testimony at the end of the case, the Derby Day should be about three weeks after the death of his sister: "Absolute ruin faced me. If I could stave things off for three weeks all would be well."

So, the case takes place in a year when there are thirteen days (three weeks minus eight days) between a moonless night in May and Derby Day. A good deal of trawling through old calendars and sports papers provides the following information:

May 1881, Moonless night = 27/05, Derby day = 01/06, Difference = 5 days
May 1882, Moonless night = 17/05, Derby day = 24/05, Difference = 7 days

May 1883, Moonless night = 06/05, Derby day = 23/05, Difference = 17 days
May 1884, Moonless night = 24/05, Derby day = 28/05, Difference = 4 days
May 1885, Moonless night = 14/05, Derby day = 03/06, Difference = 20 days
May 1886, Moonless night = 04/05, Derby day = 26/05, Difference = 22 days
May 1887, Moonless night = 22/05, Derby day = 25/05, Difference = 3 days

Examining these results, we see that 06 May 1883 is the best option for the moonless night and 23 May 1883 would be the Derby Day in question. Furthermore, Lady Beatrice died on 28 April 1883.

This doesn't work out exactly to the three weeks that Sir Robert said he needed to keep his sister's death secret, but he would have rounded the three weeks and four days down to make his crime seem slightly more palatable.

The Unpublished Cases

There are a plethora of unpublished cases mentioned in The Canon. Not all the unpublished cases can be given meaningful dates to place them on the Holmesian timeline.

Of those which can be dated, the majority are presented with a clearly stated date. There follow only the explanations of the less obvious dates and cases which deserve some extra discussion.

The Problem of the Grosvenor Square furniture van on behalf of The King of Scandinavia. (*NOBL*)

Main Action: Very early October 1887

At first glance in the text these may appear to be two separate cases. However, closer examination will reveal that they are both claimed to have happened as the last case before "The Noble Bachelor." Therefore, they are the same case. The case, then, has to squeeze in between "The Five Orange Pips" and "The Noble Bachelor."

The Second Second Stain (*NAVA*)

Main Action: July 1887

There is a case referred to in "The Naval Treaty" as The Second Stain which cannot be the same story as the 1886 "Second Stain"; the date and the details of this second Second Stain are incorrect. It is quite clearly stated as taking place in July 1887.

Holmes Engaged by the French Government (*FINA*)

Main Action: December 1890 to April 1891

We are told at the start of "The Final Problem" that Holmes has been engaged by the French government and is spending much of his time in France. However, Watson gets this information from the papers and Holmes may not have been telling them the truth. Holmes often used misinformation in the press to his advantage and this may have been a blind to put Moriarty (the focus of his attentions at this time) off guard.

The Papers of Ex-President Murillo (*NORW*)

Main Action: Sometime between 02 April and 11 August 1894

While the Ex-President Murillo referred to here is certainly the same as the one in "Wisteria Lodge," this is a separate case. We know this because there were no papers involved in "Wisteria Lodge" and this case takes place just after the Great Hiatus, not during it. The cases are likely to be connected, but they are distinct.

A Commission from the Sultan of Turkey (*BLAN*)

Main Action: Sometime between 21 and 26 January 1903

This is one of the cases Holmes has to deal with after his consultation with James Dodd but before he could help on his case.

The Case of the Abbey School (*BLAN*)

Main Action: Sometime between 21 and 26 January 1903

This is another of the cases Holmes has to deal with after his consultation with James Dodd but before he could help on his case. Some people have previously suggested that this is the same case as "The Priory School." This is not so; the names of both the school and the clients are different.

The Death of Cardinal Tosca (*BLAC*) and Wilson the Canary Trainer (*BLAC*)

Main Action: June 1895

Both of these cases are supposed to happen immediately before "Black Peter."

The Death of Crosby the Banker (*GOLD*), The Addleton Tragedy (*GOLD*), The Smith-Mortimer Succession Case (*GOLD*), and Huret, the Boulevard Assassin (*GOLD*)

Main Action: Last third of 1894

All four of these cases happen in the year 1894 but must happen after "The Norwood Builder," as all cases between the return from the Great Hiatus and "The Norwood Builder" are accounted for in the opening of that story.

The Apocrypha

There are also four apocryphal stories to consider. These are: "The Man with the Watches," "The Lost Special," "The Field Bazaar," and "How Watson Learned the Trick."

How Watson Learned the Trick

Main Action: 1922

This is a story Watson wrote for the library of Queen Mary's Dolls' House in 1922. The tone of this very short story makes it clear that it is actually a joke. Even if it were not, it would be impossible to date the story as it simply describes a conversation between Holmes and Watson.

The Field Bazaar

Main Action: Early November 1896

This is a short story which Watson wrote for an Edinburgh University fund-raising event. The conversation it describes between Holmes and Watson would, as the story makes clear, have happened shortly before the fundraiser. This places it easily in early November 1896.

The Man with the Watches and The Lost Special

Main Action: Spring 1892 and June 1890

These two stories by an unknown author do not mention Holmes by name but do mention a famous detective who puts his theories forward using phrases which sound a lot like Holmes's "when you have eliminated the impossible..." maxim. It seems clear that the detective in question is not Holmes, as his solutions turn out to be so wide of the mark. It is my contention that the detective in question is actually Watson trying his hand at detection sans Sherlock.

The Lost Special is set in June 1890. This is a period when Watson is not living at 221b. It would appear that Watson, missing the action of his bachelor days, was attempting to solve mysteries he read about in the papers.

The Man with The Watches is set in spring 1892, during the Great Hiatus. I believe this is in the period after Watson is bereaved and before Holmes returns (see my explanation for "Wisteria Lodge"). Indeed, this backs up my theory that Watson was falling to pieces as a result of that bereavement; his outlandish theory is quite, quite wrong.

WATSON'S MARRIAGES

AN ACCOUNT OF THE MANY WIVES OF WATSON

My proposed timeline has Watson getting married a good many times. While it is not possible to give exact dates when his marriages start and end, we can get a rough idea and see how frequently he was in and out of wedlock.

Generally, I make the assumption that if Watson is not living at 221b, it is because he is away being married to someone. I also assume that when Watson is living at 221b he is a bachelor (unless it is made clear otherwise). Watson gives us nice pointers every time he lives at 221b by referring to things such as "our" sitting room or page boy or whatever, so working out his weddedness is not terribly difficult.

At the start of their adventures together Holmes and Watson are clearly bachelors. After this we see Watson's marital status fluctuate as follows:

1881: Unmarried.

28 June 1887: Watson is recently married, probably in June 1887. (*NAVA*) – **Marriage 1**

September 1887: Watson is staying at 221b temporarily while his wife visits her mother. I believe this is an indication that the marriage is in trouble and this explains it ending very soon afterward. (*FIVE*)

14 October 1887: Watson is getting ready to marry in a few weeks. Marriage 1 must be over. (*NOBL*)

End of October 1887: Watson marries. (*NOBL*) – **Marriage 2**

20 March 1888: We know Watson is still in Marriage 2. (*SCAN*)

10 July 1888: Watson proposes to Mary Morstan. Marriage 2 must be over. (*SIGN*)

Late July 1888: Watson marries Mary Morstan. (*GREE*, *CARD*, and *DYIN*) – **Marriage 3**

August 1889 (After 3ʳᵈ): Marriage 3 has come to an end. (*CARD* and *DYIN*)

17 March 1890: Watson is married. (*IDEN*) – **Marriage 4**

02 April 1891: Watson is still married. Holmes is back for a few days from France and stopping with Watson. (*SILV*)

19 March 1892: Watson's fourth wife has died. Holmes returns from Hiatus to care for him. (*WIST*)

Last third of 1896: Watson is married. (*VEIL*) – **Marriage 5**

January 1897: Watson is no longer married. Marriage 5 must have ended. (*ABBE*)

September 1902: Watson has moved out of 221b but, from the amount of time he still spends there, I suspect he is not married yet. (*ILLU*, *REDC*)

January 1903: Watson has married again. (*BLAN*) – **Marriage 6**

These dates raise a couple of questions we should address.

For starters, why is it never mentioned in The Canon that Watson had so many marriages? My guess is that Watson wasn't exactly proud of his miserable matrimonial record. He doesn't hide them, but a series of six marriages, some of which are finished in a few months, is not the sort of thing he'd want to brag about.

Still, the number of his romances is not surprising. This is Jonny "Three Continents" Watson we are talking about. He was a ladies' man. But he was also a Victorian gentleman. This means if he wanted to expand his "knowledge of women," he had to do so in a socially acceptable manner.

And so to the second question: why were these marriages so short? At least four lasted less than a year. I have no idea why. Apart from the fourth marriage, I don't even know *how* they ended. Divorce was difficult in those days, so it seems unlikely. Mortality is probable, but that raises the question of why his fourth widowing was so especially traumatic for him.

Many suggestions can be put forward for why Watson's wives tended to die so quickly—Holmes poisoning them to get his chum back, Watson bringing home diseases from work, a series of fatal pregnancies because Watson makes freakishly large babies… Yes, plenty of suggestions. But that's all they can be: *suggestions*. We will never *know*.

My final question would be why did Holmes feel that marriage six was an abandonment by Watson and not the five previous wives? The only reasonable explanation is that the sixth wife was horrible. A momentary lapse of judgement led to a match in which Watson was prohibited from going on his adventures with Holmes anymore. This is borne out by the sudden decline in recorded cases. It may even explain Holmes's early retirement; without Watson to come out to play with him, London sleuthing lost its shine. It was time for him to move on.

The main thing to remember is: whatever questions are raised by Watson's marriages, none of them are insurmountable. They certainly cannot be taken to discredit my timeline. While you may find six wives in twenty-two years improbable, it is by no means impossible.

THE SHORT TIMELINE

A CHRONOLOGICAL LIST OF THE PRINCIPAL ACTION OF THE SIXTY CANONICAL CASES OF SHERLOCK HOLMES

04 May 1847 to 1865: *A Study in Scarlet*, Part II

04 February 1867 to 15 May 1867: *The Valley of Fear*, Part II

Summer 1875: "The Adventure of the *Gloria Scott*"

June 1877: "The Adventure of the Musgrave Ritual"

04 March 1881 to 05 March 1881: *A Study in Scarlet*, Part I

October 1881: "The Adventure of the Resident Patient"

05 April 1883 to 06 April 1883: "The Adventure of the Speckled Band"

05 May 1883 to 06 May 1883: "The Adventure of Shoscombe Old Place"

09 February 1884 to 10 February 1884: "The Adventure of the Beryl Coronet"

April 1884: "The Adventure of the Yellow Face"

07 January 1887 to 08 January 1887: *The Valley of Fear*, Part I

25 April 1887 to 26 April 1887: "The Adventure of the Reigate Squire"

27 July 1887 to 30 July 1887: "The Adventure of the Naval Treaty"

16 August 1887 to 17 August 1887: "The Adventure of the Crooked Man"

Late September 1887: "The Five Orange Pips"

14 October 1887: "The Adventure of the Noble Bachelor"

20 March 1888 to 22 March 1888: "A Scandal in Bohemia"

07 July 1888 to 10 July 1888: *The Sign of the Four*

July 1888 after *The Sign of the Four*: "The Adventure of the Greek Interpreter"

First half of 1889: Original crime of "The Adventure of the Veiled Lodger"

01 June 1889: "The Adventure of the Stock-Broker's Clerk"

06 June 1889 to 07 June 1889: "The Boscombe Valley Mystery"

15 June 1889 to 20 June 1889: "The Man with the Twisted Lip"

29 June 1889 to 30 June 1889: "The Adventure of the Engineer's Thumb"

August 1889: "The Adventure of the Cardboard Box"

03 August 1889: "The Adventure of the Dying Detective"

23 September 1889 to 19 October 1889: *The Hound of the Baskervilles*

17 March 1890 to 18 March 1890: "A Case of Identity"

27 June 1890: "The Red-Headed League"

27 December 1890: "The Adventure of the Blue Carbuncle"

March 1891: "The Adventure of the Copper Beeches"

02 April 1891 to 07 April 1891: "The Adventure of Silver Blaze"

24 April 1891 to 04 May 1891: "The Adventure of the Final Problem"

19 March 1892 to 24 March 1892: "The Adventure of Wisteria Lodge"

01 April 1894 to 02 April 1894: "The Adventure of the Empty House"

Autumn 1894: "The Disappearance of Lady Frances Carfax"

11 August 1894 to 12 August 1894: "The Adventure of the Norwood Builder"

15 November 1894 to 16 November 1894: "The Adventure of the Golden Pince-Nez"

15 March 1895 to 16 March 1895: "The Adventure of the Three Students"

27 April 1895 to 04 May 1895: "The Adventure of the Solitary Cyclist"

10 July 1895 to 12 July 1895: "The Adventure of Black Peter"

22 November 1895 to 23 November 1895: "The Adventure of the Bruce-Partington Plans"

04 January 1886 to 14 January 1886: "The Adventure of Charles Augustus Milverton"

Autumn 1886: "The Adventure of the Second Stain"

Last third of 1896: Main action of "The Adventure of the Veiled Lodger"

18 January 1897 to 20 January 1897: "The Adventure of the Abbey Grange"

16 March 1897 to 18 March 1897: "The Adventure of the Devil's Foot"

20 November 1897: "The Adventure of the Sussex Vampire"

13 December 1897 to 15 December 1897: "The Adventure of the Missing Three-Quarter"

27 July 1898 to 13 August 1898: "The Adventure of the Dancing Men"

04 June 1899 to 06 June 1899: "The Adventure of the Retired Colourman"

June 1900: "The Adventure of the Six Napoleons"

04 October 1900 to 06 October 1900: "The Problem of Thor Bridge"

16 May 1901 to 18 May 1901: "The Adventure of the Priory School"

26 June 1902 to 27 June 1902: "The Adventure of the Three Garridebs"

Summer 1902: "The Adventure of the Three Gables"

03 September 1902 to 15 September 1902: "The Adventure of the Illustrious Client"

24 September 1902 to 25 September 1902: "The Adventure of the Red Circle"

21 January 1903 to 26 January 1903: "The Adventure of the Blanched Soldier"

Summer 1903: "The Adventure of the Mazarin Stone"

06 September 1903 to 15 September 1903: "The Adventure of the Creeping Man"

23 July 1907 to 31 July 1907: "The Adventure of the Lion's Mane"

02 August 1914 to 03 August 1914: "His Last Bow"

THE FULL TIMELINE

A CHRONOLOGICAL LIST OF ALL THE DOINGS OF SHERLOCK HOLMES AND DR. JOHN H WATSON AND THOSE ASSOCIATED WITH THEIR CASES

1543: The original Birlstone Manor House is destroyed by a fire. (*VALL*)

1608: Birlstone Manor House is rebuilt. (*VALL*)

22 August 1642: The Great Rebellion (or English Civil War) breaks out. The original Hugo Baskerville holds Baskerville Manor. (*HOUN/MUSG*)

1647: A portrait is made of the original Hugo Baskerville. (*HOUN*)

03 September 1651: The Great Rebellion (or English Civil War) ends with Oliver Cromwell victorious. (*MUSG*)

May 1660: The English monarchy is restored in the form of King Charles II. (*MUSG*)

1670: Cheesemans, the Sussex home of Robert Ferguson, is built. (*SUSS*)

1742: A later Hugo Baskerville writes a manuscript to his sons, Rodger and John Baskerville, describing the original cause of the curse of the Baskervilles. (*HOUN*)

1810s: The last of the Roylott fortune is wasted on gambling and Stoke Moran begins to decay. (*SPEC*)

1818: Lord Mount-James is born. (*MISS*)

24 May 1819: Queen Victoria is born. (*History*)

1829: John Turner is born. (*BOSC*)

1832: Victor Trevor's father, James Armitage, is born. (*GLOR*)

1834: The death Van Jansen in Utrecht—a case which reminds Holmes of the murder in Lauriston Gardens. This is not a case Holmes was involved in. (*STUD*)

1835: Josiah Amberley is born. (*RETI*)

1836: Charles Augustus Milverton is born. (*CHAS*)

1838: Watson's father's watch is manufactured. (*SIGN*)

28 June 1838: The coronation of Queen Victoria. (*History*)

1839: Susan Cushing is born. (*CARD*)

1840: Colonel Sebastian Moran is born. (*EMPT*)

09 November 1841: King Edward VII is born. (*History*)

1842: Jonas Oldacre is born. (*NORW*)

1842: Professor Presbury is born. (*CREE*)

1845: Mary Sutherland's mother is born. (*IDEN*)

1845: "Black" Peter Carey is born. (*BLAC*)

1846: Lord Robert Walsingham de Vere St. Simon is born. (*NOBL*)

1847: Mycroft Holmes is born. (*GREE*)

04 May 1847: John and Lucy Ferrier find themselves stranded in The Great Alkali Plain, where they are rescued by the Mormons. (*STUD*)

1848: Ettie Shafter is born. (*VALL*)

1850: John Ferrier finds he is better off than his neighbours. (*STUD*)

1852: Dr. John Hamish Watson is born. (*STUD*)

1852: Neville St. Claire is born. (*TWIS*)

1853: John Ferrier finds he is well-to-do. (*STUD*)

1853: In Calcutta, Dr. Grimesby Roylott marries Mrs. Stoner (née Westphail), the mother of Helen and Julia Stoner. He is later incarcerated for the murder of his native butler. (*SPEC*)

1853: Lord Cantlemere enters official life. (*MAZA*)

06 January 1854: Sherlock Holmes is born. (*LAST*)

1855: Mrs. Amberley (maiden name unknown) is born. (*RETI*)

08 October 1855: The *Gloria Scott* leaves Falmouth. On board is James Armitage (later Trevor), a convict being transported to Australia. (*GLOR*)

06 November 1855: There is mutiny on the *Gloria Scott*, the prisoners take over. James Armitage and a few others want no further part and are set adrift in one of the *Gloria Scott*'s boats. Soon after, the *Gloria Scott* blows up. Hudson survives the wreckage and is pulled aboard James Armitage's boat. (*GLOR*)

08 November 1855: The boat of *Gloria Scott* survivors is picked up by a brig called *The Hotspur*. James Armitage changes his name to Trevor. They arrive in Australia where he makes his fortune honestly and eventually returns to England under his new identity. (*GLOR*)

1856: John Ferrier finds he is rich. (*STUD*)

1856: Effie Hebron/Munro is born. (*YELL*)

1857: A case to do with a will in Riga takes place which bears similarities to Francois Le Villard's 1888 case. This is not a case Holmes was involved in. (*SIGN*)

10 May 1857: The Indian Rebellion breaks out and Jonathan Small is caught up in it. (*SIGN*)

10 May 1857: The Indian Rebellion breaks out. Among others, Nancy Devoy, Sergeant James Barclay, and Corporal Henry Wood are shut up at Bhurtee. Both James and Henry are in love with Nancy. Nancy favours Henry. (*CROO*)

24 May 1857 – 10 pm: Henry Wood sets off to seek help on behalf of all at Bhurtee where they have run out of water. However, James Barclay has already tipped the rebels off so that they capture Henry Wood. For several years he is kept prisoner and tortured. Eventually he escapes and makes a life for himself in Punjab, preferring his friends in England to think him dead than see him disfigured. (*CROO*)

July 1857: Jonathan Small helps keep the rebelling Indians back at Shahgunge. (*SIGN*)

Late 1857/1858: Jonathan Small joins the defences at Agra Fort. (*SIGN*)

Late 1857/1858: Jonathan Small, Mahomet Singh, Abdullah Khan, and Dost Akbar kill Achmet, steal the Agra treasure and hide it in the Agra Fort. (*SIGN*)

Late 1857: After escaping from the Indian Rebellion, Sergeant (later Colonel) James Barclay marries Nancy Devoy. (*CROO*)

1858: Irene Adler is born in New Jersey (*SCAN*)

1858: Wilhelm Gottsreich Sigismond von Ormstein, the King of Bohemia is born. (*SCAN*)

1858: Twins Thaddeus and Bartholomew Sholto are born (*SIGN*)

1858: James Winter (AKA John Garrideb, Killer Evans, and Morecroft) is born. (*3GAR*)

01 November 1858: The Indian Rebellion ends and Jonathan Small, Mahomet Singh, Abdullah Khan, and Dost Akbar are arrested for the murder of Achmet. Sentenced to penal servitude, they eventually are sent to Blair Island in the Andamans. (*SIGN*)

1859: John Ferrier finds that not half a dozen men in the whole of Salt Lake City could compare with him. (*STUD*)

22 May 1859: Watson's literary agent, Arthur Ignatius Conan Doyle, is born. (*History*)

1860: James Windibank is born. (*IDEN*)

01 June 1860: Lucy Ferrier first meets Jefferson Hope. (*STUD*)

13 June 1860: Jefferson Hope leaves Salt Lake City, intending to return in August 1860 to marry Lucy Ferrier. (*STUD*)

04 July 1860: Brigham Young arrives at John Ferrier's house and demands that Lucy Ferrier marry either Enoch Drebber or Joseph Stangerson. (*STUD*)

05 July 1860: John Ferrier dispatches a note to Jefferson Hope to tell him what has happened. (*STUD*)

06 July 1860: The first of the countdown numbers (a "29") appears on John Ferrier's estate. (*STUD*)

02 August 1860: The last of the countdown numbers (a "2") appears on John Ferrier's estate. (*STUD*)

02 August 1860: Jefferson Hope arrives back in Salt Lake City and escapes with Lucy and John Ferrier. (*STUD*)

04 August 1860: While Jefferson Hope is hunting, the Mormons catch up, murder John Ferrier and abduct Lucy Ferrier. (*STUD*)

09 August 1860: Lucy Ferrier is forced to marry Enoch Dreber. (*STUD*)

10 August 1860: Jefferson Hope arrives back in Salt Lake City and discovers what has happened (*STUD*)

By 10 September 1860: Lucy Ferrier dies. (*STUD*)

1860: Baron Adelbert Gruner is born. (*ILLU*)

1860 to 1865: John Turner starts as a miner in Ballarat, Victoria, Australia but eventually becomes a highway man known as Black Jack of Ballarat. Having made his fortune, he comes to England and settles in Boscombe Valley. (*BOSC*)

1861: Mary Morstan is born. (*SIGN*)

1861: Mary Holder is born. (*BERY*)

12 April 1861: The American Civil War breaks out and Elias Openshaw serves in the Confederate Army under Thomas Jonathan "Stonewall" Jackson. (*FIVE*)

1862: Jeremiah Hayling is born. (*ENGR*)

1862: Inspector Bradstreet first joins the police force. (*TWIS*)

1863: Mr. Merryweather starts playing cards every Saturday night. (*REDH*)

1864: Victor Hatherley is born. (*ENGR*)

1864: John Horner is born. (*BLUE*)

24 June 1864: Birdy Edwards, under the name John McMurdo, joins the Society of Freemen in Chicago. (*VALL*)

1865: Mary Sutherland is born. (*IDEN*)

1865: Jefferson Hope once again returns to Salt Lake City to exact revenge but finds Enoch Dreber and Joseph Stangerson have left. (*STUD*)

1865: "La Jeune Fille a l'Agneau" by Greuze sells for one million two hundred thousand francs. (*VALL*)

09 May 1865: The American Civil War ends, and Elias Openshaw goes back to his plantation. (*FIVE*)

03 June 1865: King George V is born. (*History*)

1866: John Openshaw is born. (*FIVE*)

1866: There are incidents in Godno, Little Russia, which are analogous to the crimes in *The Hound of the Baskervilles*. This is not a case which Holmes was involved in. (*HOUN*)

1867: John Hector MacFarlane is born. (*NORW*)

04 February 1867: Birdy Edwards, under the name John McMurdo, arrives in Vermissa Valley. (*VALL*)

05 February 1867: John McMurdo tells Ettie Shafter, his landlord's daughter, he loves her. (*VALL*)

11 February 1867: John McMurdo gets in a fight with Ted Baldwin and goes to see John McGinty, where he is first introduced to the ways of the Scowrers. (*VALL*)

12 February 1867: John McMurdo moves lodgings at Jacob Shafter's insistence. (*VALL*)

02 March 1867: John McMurdo is initiated into the Scowrers. (*VALL*)

04 May 1867: John McMurdo informs the Scowrers that Pinkerton man, Birdy Edwards, is after them. John McMurdo suggests a trap for Birdy Edwards which they all agree to. (*VALL*)

05 May 1867 – 10 pm: Once he has all the important Scowrers in his home, John McMurdo reveals he is actually Birdy Edwards and they are all arrested. (*VALL*)

15 May 1867: Birdy Edwards and Ettie Shafter marry in Chicago. (*VALL*)

1868: Watson is at school with Percy "Tadpole" Phelps. (*NAVA*)

1869: Charles McCarthy catches up with John Turner in Boscombe Valley and starts blackmailing him. (*BOSC*)

04 March 1869: According to Elias Openshaw's diary, "Hudson came. Same old platform." (*FIVE*)

07 March 1869: According to Elias Openshaw's diary, "Set the pips on McCauley, Paramore and John Swain, of St Augustine." (*FIVE*)

09 March 1869: According to Elias Openshaw's diary, "McCauley cleared." (*FIVE*)

10 March 1869: According to Elias Openshaw's diary, "John Swain cleared." (*FIVE*)

12 March 1869: According to Elias Openshaw's diary, "Visited Paramore. All well." (*FIVE*)

1869/1870: Elias Openshaw comes back to England and takes a small estate in Horsham, Sussex. (*FIVE*)

1870: Ralph Smith, uncle of Violet Smith, goes to Africa to seek his fortune. (*SOLI*)

1871: James McCarthy is born. (*BOSC*)

1871: Alice Turner is born. (*BOSC*)

1871: John Hopley Neligan is born. (*BLAC*)

1871: Cecil James Barker leaves England. (*VALL*)

1871: A case to do with a will in St. Louis takes place which bears similarities to Francois Le Villard's 1888 case. This is not a case Holmes was involved in. (*SIGN*)

October 1972: Holmes starts at Oxford University. (*GLOR, MUSG*)

1872: The Duke of Holdernesse is Lord of the Admiralty. (*PRIO*)

1872: Ames, the butler, commences employment with Sir Charles Chandos. (*VALL*)

1872: There is a similar case to "The Noble Bachelor" in Munich. (*NOBL*)

June 1873: Reginald Musgrave leaves Oxford University. (*MUSG*)

1874: *Out of Doors* by J.G. Wood is published. (*LION*)

1874: Some remnant of the Scowrers gets on Birdy Edwards's trail. Under the name of John Douglas he flees to California. (*VALL*)

1874: In California, Birdy Edwards's first wife, Ettie Edwards (née Shafter) dies of typhoid. (*VALL*)

1875: Dr. Grimesby Roylott is released from prison in India and returns to England, where his wife dies in a railway accident. (*SPEC*)

1875: "Worthingdon bank business"—involving Biddle, Hayward, Moffat, and Blessington (né Sutton) (*RESI*)

1875: Cartwright, the messenger boy, is born. (*HOUN*)

1875: "Black" Peter Carey's daughter is born. (*BLAC*)

1875: Birdy Edwards, under the name John Douglas, first meets Cecil James Barker in California where they work together for five years. He must have been successful because his "luck was proverb" in 1876. (*VALL*)

25 March 1875: Dr. Percy Trevelyan is set up in practice by his resident patient, Mr. Blessington. (*RESI*)

Trinity Term 1875: Victor Trevor's bull terrier attacks Sherlock Holmes, laying him up for ten days and creating a friendship between Trevor and Holmes. (*GLOR*)

Summer 1875: While Holmes is staying at the Trevor residence in Norfolk, the main events of "The *Gloria Scott*" take place. Victor Trevor's father is blackmailed by Hudson. The incident ends with Victor Trevor's father dead and Hudson missing. The solution to the mystery is revealed by a letter from his father, rather than by Holmes. (*GLOR*)

1876: Another Rodger Baskerville, father of Rodger Baskerville (AKA Jack Stapleton), dies of yellow fever in Central America. (*HOUN*)

June 1876: Holmes leaves Oxford University and sets himself up in London. (*MUSG*)

1877: Major John Sholto retires to Pondicherry Lodge, Upper Norwood. (*SIGN*)

1877: Several of the Scowrers who were arrested in 1867 are released. (*VALL*)

1877: There is a case in Andover which is similar to "A Case of Identity." It is unclear whether Holmes was involved. (*IDEN*)

1877: Mortimer Maberley uses Holmes's services in a trifling matter. (*3GAB*)

June 1877: The main events of "The Musgrave Ritual" take place. Reginald Musgrave enlists Holmes to discover what has happened to his butler, Richard Brunton, and his maid, Rachel Howells. Holmes solves the mystery and, in the process, locates a crown that belonged to Charles I. (*MUSG*)

1878: Watson took his degree of Doctor of Medicine at London University. (*STUD*)

1878: John Openshaw first meets his uncle, Elias Openshaw. Soon after, John Openshaw moves in with his uncle. (*FIVE*)

1878: Mrs. Bernstone becomes the housekeeper at Pondicherry Lodge. (*SIGN*)

1878: Carrie Evans starts her job at Shoscombe Old Place as Lady Beatrice Falder's maid. (*SHOS*)

21 November 1878: The Second Anglo-Afghan War breaks out. (*History*)

03 December 1878: Captain Arthur Morstan arrives back in England and goes to see Major John Sholto at Pondicherry Lodge. They argue, Captain Morstan suffers a heart attack and dies. With the help of his servant, Lal Chowdar, Major Sholto disposes of Morstan's body and keeps his death secret. (*SIGN*)

03 December 1878: Mary Morstan is supposed to meet her father, Captain Arthur Morstan, in London but he does not show up. (*SIGN*)

1879: John Straker starts working as a jockey for Colonel Ross. (*SILV*)

1879: Henderson's (né Don Juan Murillo, The Tiger of San Pedro) first daughter is born. (*WIST*)

Early 1880s: The Duke of Holdernesse has an illegitimate son named James Wilder. Shortly afterwards James Wilder's mother dies. (*PRIO*)

1880: Victor Hatherley enters into apprenticeship with Venner & Matherson. (*ENGR*)

1880: Birdy Edwards, under the name John Douglas, flees California and moves to Europe. (*VALL*)

1880: In Brazil, J. Neil Gibson marries Maria Pinto. (*THOR*)

1880: Alexander Holder's brother dies. He takes his nineteen-year-old niece, Mary, in. (*BERY*)

1880: The case of Von Bischoff at Frankfort takes place, in which Von Bischoff would have been found guilty if they could have used Holmes's blood test. Other similar cases which took place an unknown time before 1881 are "Mason of Bradford," "the notorious Muller," "Lefevre of Montpellier," and "Samson of New Orleans." It is unclear whether Holmes was involved in any of these cases. (*STUD*)

27 July 1880: Battle of Maiwand, in which Doctor Watson is struck in the shoulder by a jezail bullet. (*STUD*)

01 September 1880: The Battle of Kandahar, the last major conflict of the Second Anglo-Afghan War. (*History*)

December 1880: Julia Stoner meets a major who she becomes engaged to. (*SPEC*)

1881: Colonel Sebastian Moran publishes his book *Heavy Game of the Western Himalayas*. (EMPT)

1881: Henderson's (né Don Juan Murillo, The Tiger of San Pedro) second daughter is born. (WIST)

1881: A fortnight before her wedding, Dr. Grimesby Roylott succeeds in murdering his step-daughter, Julia Stoner. (SPEC)

1881: Cecil James Barker returns to England to follow his friend John Douglas. (VALL)

1881: Birdy Edwards, under the name John Douglas, marries his second wife, Ivy Douglas. Cecil James Barker is his best man. (*VALL*)

1881: Effie Hebron marries Grant Munro. (*YELL*)

Early 1881 or Late 1880: Watson sent back from Peshawar to England on the Orontes. (*STUD*)

Early 1881 or Late 1880: Watson lands at Portsmouth jetty one month after leaving Peshawar. (*STUD*)

14 February 1881: Enoch Dreber and Joseph Stangerson take lodgings at the Charpentier residence. (*STUD*)

17 February 1881: Jefferson Hope discovers where Dreber and Stangerson are staying. (*STUD*)

Between Ontores landing and March 1881: Watson is introduced to Sherlock Holmes in St. Bart's pathology lab. (*STUD*)

03 March 1881 – 8 pm: Enoch Dreber and Joseph Stangerson leave their lodgings at the Charpentier residence. (*STUD*)

04 March 1881 – Between 12:30 am and 1 am: Jefferson Hope forces Enoch Dreber to take poison at No. 3 Lauriston Gardens. (*STUD*)

04 March 1881 – Around 2 am: Constable John Rance finds the body of Enoch Dreber. (*STUD*)

04 March 1881 – Breakfast time: Watson reads *The Book of Life* and is introduced to Holmes's occupation. (*STUD*)

04 March 1881: Mrs. Hudson asks Watson to put her terrier to sleep. Watson does not. (*STUD*)

05 March 1881 – 6 am: Joseph Stangerson is murdered by Jefferson Hope. This takes place in Halliday's Private Hotel where Stangerson has been waiting for Dreber for two days. (*STUD*)

05 March 1881: Holmes captures Jefferson Hope, gets a short confession and hands him over to Lestrade and Gregson. (*STUD*)

06 March 1881: Jefferson Hope dies when his aneurism bursts. (*STUD*)

September 1881: Mr. Blessington learns of the release of the rest of the Worthingdon Bank Gang, 9 years early. (*RESI*)

October 1881: The main events of "The Resident Patient" take place. On day one, Dr. Percy Trevelyan gets a letter from a cataleptic patient who visits him on days two and three. The cataleptic patient is in fact faking it to discover where Mr. Blessington is. On day three his resident patient is acting so strangely that he consults Holmes that evening. Early in the morning of day four the resident patient, Mr. Blessington is killed. Holmes investigates and reveals that Mr. Blessington was in fact Sutton of the Worthingdon Bank Gang and he was killed by his other gang members: Biddle, Hayward, and Moffat. (*RESI*)

1882: At sixteen, John Openshaw finds himself "quite master" of his Uncle Elias Openshaw's house. (*FIVE*)

1882: James Mortimer takes a position as house surgeon at Charing Cross Hospital. (*HOUN*)

1882: James Mortimer publishes "Some Freaks of Atavism" in the *Lancet*. (*HOUN*)

1882: Jack Ferguson is born. At this time, Robert Ferguson is married to his first wife. (*SUSS*)

1882: Birdy Edwards, under the name John Douglas, takes residence at Birlstone Manor House. (*VALL*)

1882: Ames, the butler, leaves the service of Sir Charles Chandos and commences employment with John Douglas at Birlstone Manor House. (*VALL*)

Early in 1882: Major John Sholto learns that Jonathan Small has escaped from the penal colonies of the Andaman Islands. (*SIGN*)

April 1882: Mary Morstan is employed by Mrs. Cecil Forrester as a governess. (*SIGN*)

28 April 1882: Major John Sholto dies. (*SIGN*)

04 May 1882: An advert appears in *The Times* seeking Mary Morstan. Mary responds to the advert. (*SIGN*)

04 May 1882: Mary Morstan receives her first pearl from an unknown source, which later turns out to be Thaddeus Sholto. She likely did not keep the packaging or the pearl, probably binning the one and selling the other. (*SIGN*)

September 1882: Alice Turner is sent away to boarding school. (*BOSC*)

1883: Wilhelm Gottsreich Sigismond von Ormstein, the King of Bohemia meets Irene Adler in Warsaw. They enter into a relationship. (*SCAN*)

1883: James Mortimer publishes "Do We Progress?" in the *Journal of Psychology*. (*HOUN*)

1883: "Black" Peter Carey commands the steam sealer *Sea Unicorn*. (*BLAC*)

10 March 1883: Elias Openshaw receives a letter containing five orange pips from the Ku Klux Klan. (*FIVE*)

March 1883: Helen Stoner becomes engaged to Percy Armitage. (*SPEC*)

29 March 1883: Dr. Grimesby Roylott hurls the Stoke Moran blacksmith over a parapet. (*SPEC*)

03 April 1883: Dr. Grimesby Roylott initiates building work on Helen Stoner's room so that he can move her into her sister's room and use a swamp adder to try to murder her. (*SPEC*)

05 April 1883 – 7:15 am: In fear of her life, Helen Stoner consults Holmes at 221b. After she leaves Dr. Grimesby Roylott arrives and makes some ineffective threats. (*SPEC*)

05 April 1883 – Afternoon: Holmes and Watson head to Stoke Moran. After some investigations they make plans to take Helen Stoner's place that night. (*SPEC*)

05 April 1883 – 11 pm: Holmes and Watson take Helen Stoner's place and keep vigil in her room. (*SPEC*)

06 April 1883 – 3 am: Dr. Grimesby Roylott releases a swamp adder into Helen Stoner's room. Holmes drives it back and it kills Dr. Grimesby Roylott. Holmes then explains everything. (*SPEC*)

28 April 1883: Lady Beatrice Falder dies. Sir Robert Norberton hides her corpse, intending to make people think she is still alive until after his horse runs on Derby Day. Over the next week he is seen making visits to the family crypt at night. (*SHOS*)

29 April 1883: Sir Robert Norberton gives away Lady Beatrice's dog. (*SHOS*)

May 1883: Helen Stoner is due to be married to Percy Armitage. (*SPEC*)

02 May 1883: Elias Openshaw is murdered by the Ku Klux Klan. (*FIVE*)

04 May 1883: Mary Morstan receives her second pearl from an unknown source which later turns out to be Thaddeus Sholto. Realising that this was likely to become an annual event, this is the year she began to keep the packaging and pearls. (*SIGN*)

05 May 1883: Holmes is involved is the St Pancras case in which a policeman is murdered. Holmes proves that an incriminating cap belongs to the accused man. (*SHOS*)

05 May 1883: John Mason consults Holmes at 221b regarding the strange behaviour of Lady Beatrice Falder and Sir Robert Norberton at Shoscombe Old Place. (*SHOS*)

05 May 1883 – Evening: Holmes and Watson travel to Shoscombe Old Place to investigate John Mason's concerns. (*SHOS*)

06 May 1883: Holmes and Watson investigate at Shoscombe Old Place and the family crypt. They meet Sir Robert Norberton. Holmes states all that he knows, and Sir Robert Norberton fills in the rest of the mystery. (*SHOS*)

23 May 1883: Derby Day. Shoscombe Prince runs and wins his race. (*SHOS*)

August 1883: The Neligan and Dawson bank fails. Mr. Neligan takes some securities and sets off for Norway to realise them in order to pay off his creditors. (*BLAC*)

August 1883: Having been blown off course, Mr. Neligan is rescued from his yacht by the crew of the *Sea Unicorn*. On the second night after his rescue, "Black" Peter Carey throws Mr. Neligan overboard and steals his securities. Patrick Cairns witnesses this. (*BLAC*)

1884: Colonel Sebastian Moran publishes his book *Three Months in the Jungle*. (*EMPT*)

1884: Hatty Doran meets Francis H. Moulton in McQuires Camp near the Rockies. (*NOBL*)

1884: Holmes fights three rounds with McMurdo the prize-fighter on the night of his benefit. (*SIGN*)

1884: John Straker starts working at Colonel Ross's stables as a trainer. (*SILV*)

1884: James Mortimer marries, leaves Charing Cross Hospital and sets up his own home in Dartmoor where he becomes Medical Officer for Grimpen, Thorsley, and High Barrow. (*HOUN*)

1884: "Black" Peter Carey retires and begins travelling. (*BLAC*)

1884: John Douglas has a hunting accident that leaves him delirious with a fever. (*VALL*)

1884: Hall Pycroft starts work for Coxon and Woodhouse's. (*STOC*)

1884: The Beddington brothers are jailed. (*STOC*)

January 1884: Joseph Openshaw inherits and moves in to Elias Openshaw's home in Horsham. (*FIVE*)

08 February 1884 – Morning: At his bank, Alexander Holder takes a beryl coronet as security for a large loan to an eminent nobleman. (*BERY*)

09 February 1884 – 2 am: Alexander Holder's niece, Mary Holder, steals the beryl coronet and gives it to her lover, Sir George Burnwell. Alexander's son Arthur Holder sees this and tries to rescue the beryl coronet. He only succeeds in getting most of it. Part is stolen away by George Burnwell. Alexander Holder comes in to see his son with what remains and assumes he has stolen it and hidden the missing part. Arthur huffily refuses to tell what happened and ends up arrested. (*BERY*)

09 February 1884 – Morning: Alexander Holder consults Holmes about the theft of the beryl coronet which was in his care. Holmes spends the rest of the day investigating. (*BERY*)

09 February 1884 – Late at night: Holmes meets Sir George Burnwell, makes it known that he knows all and purchases the remainder of the beryl coronet from Burnwell's fence. (*BERY*)

10 February 1884 – Morning: Mary Holder and Sir George Burnwell run away together. (*BERY*)

10 February 1884 – 9 am: Alexander Holder returns to 221b. Holmes reveals all and sells the remainder of the beryl coronet back to Alexander Holder. (*BERY*)

11 February 1884: The beryl coronet is due to be reclaimed by the eminent nobleman who borrowed against it. (*BERY*)

March 1884: Effie Munro asks her husband for money which she uses to secretly bring her daughter, Lucy, to a nearby cottage in England. Her husband, Grant Munro, knows nothing of the daughter or the way the money was spent. (*YELL*)

April 1884: The main events of "The Yellow Face" take place. One Saturday, Grant Munro consults Holmes about his wife's unusual behaviour. Holmes expects a different outcome to the one he gets but the case is solved the same day. (*YELL*)

May 1884: Neville St. Claire moves to Lee, Kent. (*TWIS*)

04 May 1884: Mary Morstan receives her third pearl from an unknown source, which later turns out to be Thaddeus Sholto. (*SIGN*)

1885: Under the name Vandeleur, Jack and Beryl Stapleton run St. Oliver's private school. (*HOUN*)

1885: Bannister takes employment as Hilton Soames's servant. (*3STU*)

1885: Cadogen West enters into employment at Woolwich Arsenal. (*BRUC*)

January 1885: The *Lone Star* is docked in Dundee. (*FIVE*)

04 January 1885: Joseph Openshaw receives the five orange pips from the Ku Klux Klan. (*FIVE*)

07 January 1885: Joseph Openshaw goes to stay with his friend Major Freebody on Portsdown Hill, Portsmouth, Hampshire. (*FIVE*)

08 January 1885 – about 4 pm: Joseph Openshaw has a fatal fall into a deep chalk pit because he is attacked by the Ku Klux Klan. (*FIVE*)

09 January 1885: John Openshaw receives a telegram from Major Freebody informing him that his father, Joseph Openshaw, has had a fall. John rushes to see him but he dies before John arrives. (*FIVE*)

04 May 1885: Mary Morstan receives her fourth pearl from an unknown source, which later turns out to be Thaddeus Sholto. (*SIGN*)

1886: Hatty Doran and Lord Robert Walsingham de Vere St. Simon meet in San Francisco. (*NOBL*)

1886: Silver Blaze is born. (*SILV*)

1886: Under the name Henderson, Don Juan Murillo, The Tiger of San Pedro, arrives in England where he will hide at High Gable near Oxshott. (*WIST*)

03 January 1886: Lady Eva Blackwell is being blackmailed by Charles Augustus Milverton and commissions Holmes to act as her agent with him. (*CHAS*)

04 January 1886 – 6 pm: Holmes and Watson return to 221b after a walk to find a card from Charles Augustus Milverton saying that he will call to speak to Holmes about the blackmailing of Lady Eva Blackwell. (*CHAS*)

05 to 13 January 1886: Holmes, masquerading as a plumber named Escott, courts Agatha, one of Milverton's maids, and eventually becomes engaged to her. This is all so that he can learn Charles Augustus Milverton's habits and the layout of his home. (*CHAS*)

13 January 1886 – Evening: Returning to 221b, Holmes explains what he has been doing to Watson. Between them, they make plans to break into Appledore Towers, the home of Charles Augustus Milverton; so that they can retrieve the letters he is using to blackmail Lady Eva Blackwell. (*CHAS*)

13 January 1886 – 11 pm: Holmes and Watson break into Appledore Towers and are in the process of cracking Charles Augustus Milverton's safe when they are interrupted by Charles Augustus Milverton, who receives an unknown guest. The guest turns out to be a woman Milverton had previously blackmailed. She exacts revenge by shooting Milverton four times. She escapes but the alarm is raised. Holmes burns the contents of the safe and Watson and Holmes escape, too. (*CHAS*)

14 January 1886 – Morning: Inspector Lestrade comes to 221b to ask Holmes for help solving the murder of Charles Augustus Milverton. Holmes declines. (*CHAS*)

04 May 1886: Mary Morstan receives her fifth pearl from an unknown source, which later turns out to be Thaddeus Sholto. (*SIGN*)

Autumn 1886: At some point the main events of "The Second Stain" take place. Holmes is consulted by Lord Bellinger and The Right Honourable Trelawney Hope with regards to an important document which has gone missing. Four days later he has retrieved and returned the document. (*SECO*)

November 1886: Hatty Doran is brought over to England by her father for the London season. (*NOBL*)

1887: James McCarthy marries a barmaid in Bristol. He does not know that the barmaid is already married so the marriage is not legitimate. (*BOSC*)

1887: Neville St. Claire marries Mrs. St. Claire, the daughter of a Lee brewer. (*TWIS*)

1887: Victor Hatherley's father dies. He uses his inheritance to start in business for himself. (*ENGR*)

1887: Sir Charles Baskerville returns to England to take his seat at Baskerville Hall. (*HOUN*)

1887: Jack and Beryl Stapleton take residence in Merripit House, shortly after Sir Charles Baskerville arrives at Baskerville Hall. (*HOUN*)

1887: Henry Baker was still well-to-do. (*BLUE*)

1887: Mr. and Mrs. Warren move into their home in Bloomsbury. (*REDC*)

1887: Holmes and Watson are involved in the adventure of the Paradol Chamber. (*FIVE*)

1887: Holmes and Watson are involved in the adventure of the Amateur Mendicant Society, who held a luxurious club in the lower vault of a furniture warehouse. (*FIVE*)

1887: Holmes and Watson are investigating the loss of the British barque *Sophy Anderson*. (*FIVE*)

1887: Holmes and Watson are involved in the singular adventures of the Grice Patersons in the island of Uffa. (*FIVE*)

1887: Holmes and Watson investigate the Camberwell poisoning case in which Sherlock Holmes was able, by winding up the dead man's watch, to prove that it had been wound up two hours before, and that therefore the deceased had gone to bed within that time. (*FIVE*)

1887: Bert Stevens wants Holmes to get him off a murder charge, but Holmes concludes he is guilty. (*NORW*)

1887: Colonel Sebastian Moran murders Mrs. Stewart of Lauder. Holmes tries but fails to prove Moran's guilt. (*EMPT*)

05 January 1887: Ted Baldwin, under the name Hargrave, takes a room at the Eagle Commercial in Tunbridge Wells. (*VALL*)

05 January 1887: While shopping in Tunbridge Wells, John Douglas catches a glimpse of Ted Baldwin. He keeps his fears secret but several around him notice how nervous he has become. (*VALL*)

06 January 1887 – Morning: Ted Baldwin sets off for Birlstone Manor House on a bicycle. (*VALL*)

06 January 1887 – Afternoon: Ivy Douglas has visitors to tea at Birlstone Manor House. They leave around 6 pm. (*VALL*)

06 January 1887 – 6 pm: The drawbridge at Birlstone Manor House is raised. (*VALL*)

06 January 1887 – 11:30 pm: John Douglas appears to have been murdered. (*VALL*)

07 January 1887 – 12 am: Police arrive on the scene of the Birlstone Manor House murder. (*VALL*)

07 January 1887 – 3 am: Sussex police detective White Mason arrives at Birlstone Manor House to investigate the murder. (*VALL*)

07 January 1887 – 5:40 am: White Mason sends for help from Scotland Yard. (*VALL*)

07 January 1887 – Morning: Holmes receives the first of two letters from Porlock. It is a cipher warning of the tragedy at Birlstone House. Shortly after Holmes and Watson break the cipher, Inspector Alec MacDonald arrives at 221b to ask for his help solving the apparent murder of John Douglas at Birlstone Manor House. (*VALL*)

07 January 1887 – 12 pm: Holmes, Watson, and Inspector Alec MacDonald meet White Mason at Birlstone station. Holmes starts his investigations. (*VALL*)

08 January 1887 – 4 pm: Holmes reveals that the corpse is not John Douglas. He locates John Douglas who tells his story. (*VALL*)

February 1887: Ivy Douglas and John Douglas are forced to flee England and take a ship to Cape Town, South Africa. (*VALL*)

Early March 1887: Holmes and Watson receive news from Ivy Douglas that Moriarty had caught up with Birdy Edwards and Edwards had been killed and thrown overboard on the ship to Cape Town. (*VALL*)

March and half of April 1887: Holmes investigates the affair of the Netherland-Sumatra company and the colossal schemes of Baron Maupertuis. (*REIG*)

14 April 1887: Watson receives a telegram telling him Holmes is sick in the Hotel Dulong, Lyons. (*REIG*)

15 April 1887: Watson arrives in Lyons to minister Holmes. (*REIG*)

18 April 1887: Holmes and Watson return to Baker Street. (*REIG*)

18 April 1887: Cunningham Senior and Cunningham Junior break in to Old Acton's to steal some paperwork. They are seen doing this by their own coachman, William Kirwan. (*REIG*)

25 April 1887: Holmes and Watson go to stay with Colonel Hayter in Reigate. (*REIG*)

25 April 1887 – 11:45 pm: The alarm is raised when William Kirwan is shot by Cunninghams Senior and Junior (*REIG*)

26 April 1887 – Breakfast time: Colonel Hayter's butler tells Hayter, Holmes, and Watson that William Kirwan has been murdered. Inspector Forrester then asks for Holmes's help. (*REIG*)

26 April 1887 – Morning: Holmes travels to the Cunninghams' house and proves that they murdered William Kirwan. (*REIG*)

04 May 1887: Mary Morstan receives her sixth pearl from an unknown source, which later turns out to be Thaddeus Sholto. (*SIGN*)

23 May 1887 – Working day: In his job at the Foreign Office, Lord Holdhurst, his uncle, asks Percy Phelps to remain late that evening to make a copy of a secret naval treaty. (*NAVA*)

23 May 1887 – Early evening: After going out to dine, Percy Phelps returns to the office to begin work copying out the secret naval treaty. (*NAVA*)

23 May 1887 – 9 pm: Having got as far as copying nine of the twenty-six articles in the naval treaty, Percy Phelps asks the commissionaire for some coffee. Later, when it has not come, he goes to check where it is. (*NAVA*)

23 May 1887 – 9:45 pm: Joseph Harrison arrives at Percy Phelps's office to see his friend. Finding the office empty, he opportunistically steals the secret naval treaty and departs for Briarbrae. When he gets there, he hides the naval treaty in the guest room he is occupying. (*NAVA*)

23 May 1887 – 10 pm: While he checks on the commissionaire, Percy Phelps hears the bell from his office being rung, he rushes back to find the treaty has been stolen. After initial enquiries reveal no trace of the treaty, Percy Phelps returns home to Briarbrae and suffers such a brain fever that he has to be put up in the ground floor guest room, which Joseph Harrison had been occupying. (*NAVA*)

20 June 1887: Queen Victoria's Golden Jubilee (*History*)

July 1887: Holmes and Watson are involved in a different case to "The Second Stain," which is also called The Second Stain. (*NAVA*)

July 1887: Watson and Holmes are involved in the Adventure of the Tired Captain. (*NAVA*)

27 July 1887: Percy Phelps recovers enough from his brain fever to be able to send a letter to Watson asking for his and Holmes's help. (*NAVA*)

28 July 1887 – Morning: Using chemistry, Holmes solves a commonplace little murder case. (*NAVA*)

28 July 1887 – Morning: Watson receives a letter from Percy "Tadpole" Phelps imploring him to bring Holmes to his home, Briarbrae, in Woking. (*NAVA*)

28 July 1887 – Morning: Watson and Holmes arrive at Briarbrae and Percy Phelps explains about the theft of the naval treaty. (*NAVA*)

28 July 1887 – 3:20 pm: Watson and Holmes return to London to conduct their investigations. (*NAVA*)

29 July 1887 – 2 am: Joseph Harrison tries to retrieve the stolen naval treaty from Percy Phelps's sick room. However, when Percy Phelps wakes up, he is forced to run off before he can be recognised. (*NAVA*)

29 July 1887 – Morning: Holmes and Watson return to Briarbrae and Percy Phelps tells them of the events the previous night. (*NAVA*)

29 July 1887 – Early afternoon: Holmes sets everything up to trap Joseph Harrison: Watson and Phelps travel to 221b where they spend the night. Holmes makes it appear to all that he is going too, but secretly remains in Woking. (*NAVA*)

29 July 1887 – 8 pm: Holmes stakes out Percy Phelps's empty sick room at Briarbrae, Woking. (*NAVA*)

30 July 1887 – 2 am: Holmes catches Joseph Harrison in the act of trying to retrieve the stolen naval treaty. Holmes manages to get the papers but Joseph Harrison escapes. Holmes then wires all the details to Inspector Forbes at Scotland Yard. (*NAVA*)

30 July 1887 – 8 am: Holmes arrives back at 221b. He theatrically returns the naval treaty to Percy Phelps and then explains all. (*NAVA*)

15 August 1887 – 7:30 pm: Nancy Barclay and her friend, Miss Morrison, set off for a meeting of The Guild of St. George. (*CROO*)

15 August 1887 – 8 pm: Nancy Barclay and her friend, Miss Morrison, attend the meeting of The Guild of St. George. (*CROO*)

15 August 1887 – 8:40 pm: Nancy Barclay and her friend, Miss Morrison, leave the meeting of The Guild of St. George. (*CROO*)

15 August 1887 – 8:45 pm: Nancy Barclay and Miss Morrison bump into Henry Wood. Nancy Barclay parts from Miss Morrison and Henry Wood explains to Nancy Barclay how James Barclay betrayed him thirty years earlier. (*CROO*)

15 August 1887 – 9:15 pm: Nancy Barclay returns home from the meeting of The Guild of St. George. Soon after she is in argument with Colonel James Barclay regarding his treachery towards Henry Wood thirty years previously. (*CROO*)

15 August 1887 – 9:25 pm: When a maid brings Colonel James Barclay and his wife Nancy Barclay tea, she hears that they are having a loud argument and fails to gain access to the room. (*CROO*)

15 August 1887 – 9:35 pm: From their garden, Henry Wood approaches the room where James and Nancy Barclay are arguing. He intends to confront James Barclay, but as soon as James Barclay sees Henry Wood, he has a stroke and dies. The servants hear Nancy Barclay scream and James Barclay collapse. Henry Wood flees the scene. When the servants enter the room, they find Nancy Barclay suffering brain fever and James Barclay dead. All assume Nancy has murdered her husband. (*CROO*)

16 August 1887 – Morning: Major Murphy (Colonel James Barclay's officer) summons Holmes to Aldershot to investigate the death of Colonel James Barclay. (*CROO*)

16 August 1887: After a day of investigation, Holmes discovers Henry Wood is involved and he needs to speak to him. (*CROO*)

16 August 1887 – 11:45 pm: Holmes turns up at Watson's home, asks for Watson's help with the Barclay case and a bed for the night. Before retiring, Holmes lays all the facts before Watson. (*CROO*)

17 August 1887: Holmes and Watson travel to Aldershot and speak to Henry Wood. He tells them the whole story. They all decide there is no need to tell anyone what happened unless the blame falls on Nancy Barclay. On their way to the train station Holmes and Watson meet Major Murphy, who tells them the medical inquest has proven James Barclay died of a stroke so the case can be dropped. (*CROO*)

Late September 1887: The main action of "The Five Orange Pips" takes place. On day one, John Openshaw receives the five orange pips from the Ku Klux Klan. One day two, Major Prendergast advises John Openshaw to consult Sherlock Holmes, which he does. Despite Holmes advising John Openshaw on how to proceed, between 9 pm and 10 pm, John Openshaw is drowned by the Ku Klux Klan. Holmes then goes on to solve the case. (*FIVE*)

Sometime between September and December 1887: The *Lone Star* sinks and all hands are presumed dead. (*FIVE*)

Very early October 1887: Holmes clears up the little problem of the Grosvenor Square furniture van on behalf of The King of Scandinavia (*NOBL*)

04 October 1887: Francis H. Moulton settles his bill at a select Northumberland Avenue hotel. (*NOBL*)

11 October 1887: The wedding of Hatty Doran and Lord Robert Walsingham de Vere St. Simon. (*NOBL*)

11 October 1887: Flora Millar interrupts the reception following Hatty Doran and Lord St. Simon's wedding. (*NOBL*)

11 October 1887: Hatty Doran runs off with Francis H. Moulton during her wedding breakfast. She leaves no indication where she has gone for Lord St. Simon. (*NOBL*)

12 October 1887: The wedding of Hatty Doran and Lord Robert Walsingham de Vere St. Simon is announced in the papers. (*NOBL*)

13 October 1887: The disappearance of Hatty Doran is reported in the papers. (*NOBL*)

14 October 1887 – 4 pm: Lord St. Simon consults Sherlock Holmes. (*NOBL*)

14 October 1887 – 5 pm: While Holmes is out, Watson receives delivery of a fancy meal at 221b Baker Street. (*NOBL*)

14 October 1887 – 9 pm: Francis Moulton, Hatty Doran, Lord St. Simon, Holmes, and Watson meet at 221b Baker Street and Holmes explains what has happened. (*NOBL*)

November 1887: *A Study in Scarlet* is first published publicly. (*STUD*)

Early 1888: Holmes is of service to one of the Royal houses of Europe. (*SCAN*)

1888: The Duke of Holdernesse marries Edith Appledore. (*PRIO*)

15 March 1888: Watson goes for a country walk and comes home terribly messy. (*SCAN*)

20 March 1888 – 7:45 pm: Watson arrives at 221b and is followed shortly after by Wilhelm Gottsreich Sigismond von Ormstein, the King of Bohemia who consults Sherlock Holmes. (*SCAN*)

21 March 1888 – 11:57 am: Irene Adler marries Godfrey Norton with Sherlock Holmes in disguise acting as witness. (*SCAN*)

21 March 1888 – 4 pm: Holmes meets Watson at 221b, and they discuss the King of Bohemia's case. (*SCAN*)

21 March 1888 – 6:50 pm: At Briony Lodge Holmes, Watson and a cast of helpers trick Irene Adler into revealing the location of her hiding place, which contains the letters and photograph the King wishes to recover. (*SCAN*)

22 March 1888 – 12 am: Irene Adler writes a letter for Holmes and the King of Bohemia and leaves it in her hiding place at Briony Lodge. (*SCAN*)

22 March 1888 – 5:15 am: Irene Adler and Godfrey Norton escape to the continent. (*SCAN*)

22 March 1888 – 8 am: Holmes, Watson, and the King of Bohemia arrive at Briony Lodge to find Irene Adler has gone and left them a letter. (*SCAN*)

26 March 1888: The engagement of Wilhelm Gottsreich Sigismond von Ormstein, the King of Bohemia, and Clotilde Lothman von Saxe-Meningen is officially announced. (*SCAN*)

April 1888: One of the "many months" of stagnation which lead to Holmes using cocaine. (*SIGN*)

May 1888: Another of the "many months" of stagnation which lead to Holmes using cocaine. (*SIGN*)

04 May 1888: Mary Morstan receives her seventh pearl from an unknown source, which later turns out to be Thaddeus Sholto. (*SIGN*)

June 1888: Another of the "many months" of stagnation which lead to Holmes using cocaine. (*SIGN*)

July 1888: Holmes investigates the Manor House case and proves Adams was responsible. (*GREE*)

Week commencing Sunday 01 July 1888: Holmes is consulted by Francois Le Villard regarding a case revolving around a will. (*SIGN*)

06 July 1888: Thaddeus Sholto discovers that Bartholomew Sholto has found the Agra Treasure hidden in Pondicherry Lodge. He leaves Pondicherry Lodge at 10 pm. (*SIGN*)

07 July 1888 – Morning: Holmes receives a letter of praise from Francois Le Villard for his assistance in a case the previous week. (*SIGN*)

07 July 1888 – Morning: Mordecai Smith sets off with Jonathan Small and Tonga on the *Aurora*. (*SIGN*)

07 July 1888 – Morning: Mary Morstan receives Thaddeus Sholto's anonymous letter, asking her to be at the Lyceum that evening with two friends. (*SIGN*)

07 July 1888 – 7 pm: Mary Morstan, Holmes, and Watson are met at the third pillar from the left of the Lyceum Theatre by Williams, who takes them to the home of Thaddeus Sholto. Thaddeus

Sholto acquaints them with some details of the history of the Agra Treasure and what happened to Captain Arthur Morstan. (*SIGN*)

07 July 1888 – 11 pm: Mrs. Bernstone sees the corpse of Bartholomew Sholto through the keyhole. (*SIGN*)

07 July 1888 – 11 pm: Mary Morstan, Thaddeus Sholto, Holmes, and Watson make their way to Pondicherry Lodge and discover the corpse of Bartholomew Sholto. (*SIGN*)

08 July 1888 – 1 am: Watson takes Mary Morstan home. She gets there at 2 am. He collects Toby from Sherman and returns to Pondicherry Lodge at 3 am. Toby leads them to the premises of Mordecai Smith. (*SIGN*)

08 July 1888: Mordecai Smith places the *Aurora* in dry dock at Jacobson's. Mordecai Smith, Jonathan Small, and Tonga go into hiding. (*SIGN*)

08 July 1888: Holmes calls in the help of the Baker Street Irregulars to track down the *Aurora*. (*SIGN*)

10 July 1888: Holmes's advert seeking Mordecai Smith appears in papers. (*SIGN*)

10 July 1888 – 8 pm: Athelney Jones, Holmes, and Watson pursue the *Aurora* down the Thames, eventually overtaking her and capturing Jonathan Small. In the chase Tonga is killed and the treasure is thrown overboard. (*SIGN*)

10 July 1888 – late evening: Watson proposes to Mary Morstan, who accepts. (*SIGN*)

July 1888 between 11th and 31st: The main events of "The Greek Interpreter" take place in one evening. Watson is introduced to Mycroft Holmes at the Diogenes Club. Holmes and Watson are told about Mr. Melas's encounter of two days ago (he meets Sophy Kratides and two villains who are holding Paul Kratides hostage). They get information in a letter from J. Davenport and figure out what has happened. Mr. Melas is kidnapped and an attempt is made on his life. Paul Kratides dies in the same attempt. Mr. Melas is rescued by Holmes and Watson but the villains escape with Sophy Kratides. (*GREE*)

Late July 1888: Watson marries Mary Morstan. (*GREE*, *CARD*, and *DYIN*)

09 August 1888 – Evening: Jeremiah Haying is murdered by "Colonel Lysander Stark." (*ENGR*)

Late 1888: In Buda-Pesth, the two villains of "The Greek Interpreter" are killed by Sophy Kratides. (*GREE*)

1889: There is a similar case to "A Case of Identity" in The Hague. It is unclear whether Holmes was involved. (*IDEN*)

1889: "Black" Peter Carey moves to Woodman's Lee, Sussex. (*BLAC*)

1889: Helen Stoner dies. (*SPEC*)

1889: Watson writes up the story of "The Speckled Band," although it is not published publicly for another three years. (*SPEC*)

1889: Henry "Holy" Peters is bitten in a saloon fight in Adelaide resulting in a disfigured ear. (*LADY*)

Early 1889: The Beddington brothers are released from jail. (*STOC*)

At some point in the first six months of 1889: The Abbas Parva Tragedy takes place. Leonardo the Strongman and Mrs. Eugenia Ronder plot to kill Mr. Ronder. While Mr. Ronder is killed, Leonardo abandons Eugenia Ronder to be disfigured by a circus lion. Holmes is asked for his help, but he makes no progress. (*VEIL*)

Spring 1889: Coxon & Woodhouse hit financial difficulties. As a result, Hall Pycroft and twenty-six others lose their jobs with them. (*STOC*)

13 April 1889: James Mortimer reports already seeing signs that Sir Charles Baskerville was afraid of the legend of the Hound of the Baskervilles. (*HOUN*)

04 May 1889: Sir Charles Baskerville, under the advice of James Mortimer, decides to travel to London on 05 May 1889, but that evening is chased by the Hound and dies of heart failure. (*HOUN*)

05 May 1889 – 12 am: Barrymore, the butler, discovers the body of Sir Charles Baskerville. (*HOUN*)

14 May 1889: An account of Sir Charles Baskerville's death appears in the *Devon County Chronicle*. (*HOUN*)

24 May 1889 – Afternoon: Hall Pycroft is offered a job at Mawson and Williams if he shows up on Monday 27 May 1889. (*STOC*)

24 May 1889 – Evening: Hall Pycroft is approached by the first of the two Beddington brothers in the guise of Arthur Pinner. He is offered a better job in Birmingham, which he accepts. (*STOC*)

25 May 1889 – 1 pm: Hall Pycroft arrives in Birmingham for his job with the Franco-Midland Hardware Company. He is met by the first Beddington brother, who is now pretending to be Harry Pinner. He is put to menial work for the next six days. (*STOC*)

26 May 1889: Watson is suffering from a summer cold. (*STOC*)

27 May 1889: Posing as Hall Pycroft, the second of the two Beddington brothers takes his job at Mawson and Williams. (*STOC*)

31 May 1889: James McCarthy goes to Bristol to visit the barmaid he thinks is his wife. (*BOSC*)

31 May 1889: Hall Pycroft becomes suspicious of the Franco-Midland Hardware Company when he notices that Harry and Arthur Pinner have identical fillings. That evening he takes a night train to consult Holmes. (*STOC*)

Early June 1889: Holmes is involved in the Dundas separation case, in which Mr. Dundas had drifted into the habit of winding up every meal by taking out his false teeth and hurling them at his wife. (*IDEN*)

01 June 1889 – Morning: Hall Pycroft arrives at 221b and requests Holmes's help figuring out what is going on with the Franco-Midland Hardware Company. (*STOC*)

01 June 1889 – Morning: Holmes visits Watson to ask him to accompany him to Birmingham to investigate the business of the Stock-Broker's Clerk. (*STOC*)

01 June 1889 – 12 pm: Mawson and Williams closes for the day. (*STOC*)

01 June 1889 – 1 pm: The second Beddington brother returns to the office of Mawson and Williams, kills the watchman, steals a hundred thousand pounds' worth of American railway bonds and is caught by police officers leaving the building at 1:20 pm. (*STOC*)

01 June 1889 – Just before 7 pm: The first Beddington brother reads in the paper about the capture of the other that afternoon. (*STOC*)

01 June 1889 – 7 pm: Holmes, Watson, and Hall Pycroft arrive at the offices of the Franco-Midland Hardware Company intending to investigate. However, as they arrive "Harry Pinner" leaves the room and tries to hang himself. He is saved, Holmes figures everything out and explains all. (*STOC*)

03 June 1889: James McCarthy returns from visiting the woman he thinks is his wife in Bristol. (*BOSC*)

03 June 1889: Charles McCarthy is murdered by John Turner near the Boscombe Pool. (*BOSC*)

03 June 1889: James McCarthy is arrested for the murder of Charles McCarthy. (BOSC)

04 June 1889: Alice Turner asks Inspector Lestrade to investigate the Boscombe Valley case on behalf of James McCarthy. (*BOSC*)

05 June 1889: Inspector Lestrade investigates the Boscombe Valley case and then recommends calling in Holmes. (*BOSC*)

06 June 1889 – 11:15 am: The Boscombe Valley Mystery is referred to Holmes. Holmes and Watson travel to Boscombe Valley and make preliminary enquiries. (*BOSC*)

07 June 1889 – 9 am: Lestrade, Watson, and Holmes investigate the McCarthy home of Hatherley Farm and the Boscombe Pool. (*BOSC*)

07 June 1889 – Afternoon: John Turner comes to see Watson and Holmes at their hotel. He confesses to the murder of Charles McCarthy, explains their history and signs a confession in case it is needed. (*BOSC*)

15 June 1889 – 4:35 pm: Mrs. St. Claire sees her husband in the window of the Bar of Gold. He then goes missing. (*TWIS*)

15 June 1889 – 4:45 pm: Neville St. Claire pens a letter to his wife to reassure her all is well. He hands it to the Lascar to post but the Lascar doesn't get to post it immediately. (*TWIS*)

17 June 1889: Isa Whitney goes to the Bar of Gold to smoke opium. (*TWIS*)

19 June 1889: Neville St. Claire's letter is posted and received by Mrs. St. Claire. (*TWIS*)

19 June 1889 – Evening: Kate Whitney appears at the home of Watson to ask for his help getting Isa Whitney back home. (*TWIS*)

19 June 1889 – 11 pm: At the Bar of Gold, Watson sends Isa Whitney home in a cab and then meets Sherlock Holmes, who is in disguise seeking Neville St. Claire. (*TWIS*)

20 June 1889 – 4:25 am: After a night of cogitating, Holmes solves the case, wakes Watson, and with Inspector Bradstreet they go to the cell of Hugh Boone to reveal that he is actually Neville St. Claire. (*TWIS*)

29 June 1889 – Morning: Fritz, using the name Colonel Lysander Stark, employs Victor Hatherley to provide consultation on his hydraulic equipment. (*ENGR*)

29 June 1889 – Late evening: Victor Hatherley arrives at the home of Colonel Lysander Stark. After Victor works on the hydraulic press, the Colonel tries to kill him. Victor loses a thumb, manages to escape and then faints. (*ENGR*)

29 June 1889 – Late evening: The house of "Dr. Becher" and "Lysander Stark" catches fire due to a lamp which was smashed as Victor Hatherley made his escape. (*ENGR*)

30 June 1889 – Dawn: Victor Hatherley wakes near Eyford Station. (*ENGR*)

30 June 1889 – 4:45 am: Victor Hatherley boards a train for Paddington at Eyford Station. (*ENGR*)

30 June 1889 – 6 am: Victor Hatherley arrives in London, is ministered to by Watson and then taken around to see Holmes. (*ENGR*)

30 June 1889 – Afternoon: Victor Hatherley, Inspector Bradstreet, Holmes, and Watson return to Eyford to arrest "Dr. Becher" and "Colonel Lysander Stark," only to find they have fled and the house is on fire. (*ENGR*)

15 July 1889: James McCarthy is acquitted at the Herefordshire summer assizes. (*BOSC*)

31 July 1889: Culverton Smith becomes aware that Holmes is looking into Smith's murder of Victor Savage. Culverton Smith sends Holmes a trick box to infect him with a deadly disease. Holmes realises what the box is and does not open it. He then starts pretending to be ill as part of a plan to catch Culverton Smith. (*DYIN*)

03 August 1889 – 4 pm: Mrs. Hudson asks Watson to come to 221b to treat Holmes, who appears to have been dying for three days. When he arrives, Holmes refuses treatment and keeps Watson captive for two hours. (*DYIN*)

03 August 1889 – 6 pm: Holmes sends Watson to fetch Culverton Smith. With Watson hidden as a witness, Holmes tricks Culverton Smith into admitting he killed Victor Savage and attempted to kill Holmes. The police arrive, Culverton Smith is arrested. Holmes explains all. (*DYIN*)

August 1889 after 3rd: The main action of "The Cardboard Box" takes place. Jim Browner returns home to find his wife Mary with Alec Fairbairn. In a rage, he kills them both, cuts off their ears and posts them to Sarah Cushing, but uses the wrong address. A few days later Susan Cushing receives the ears of Mary Browner and Alec Fairbairn in the post. The following day, Inspector Lestrade asks for Holmes's assistance in the case. By the evening of the next day, Holmes has solved the case, Jim Browner is arrested and Holmes reveals all. (*CARD*)

Last half of 1889: Six months after The Abbas Parva Tragedy, Mrs. Ronder recovers sufficiently to hide away in lodgings with Mrs. Merrilow. (*VEIL*)

September 1889: Holmes deals with a blackmailing case on behalf of one of the most revered names in England. (*HOUN*)

23 September 1889: James Mortimer visits 221b to consult Holmes. Finding Holmes is out, he waits a while and then leaves, forgetting to take his walking stick. (*HOUN*)

24 September 1889 – 9 am: James Mortimer returns to 221b, with his curly haired spaniel, to consult Holmes over what to do with Sir Henry Baskerville. (*HOUN*)

24 September 1889 – 10 am: James Mortimer leaves 221b to meet Sir Henry Baskerville at Waterloo Station. (*HOUN*)

24 September 1889: Sir Henry Baskerville takes rooms at Northumberland Hotel. (*HOUN*)

24 September 1889 – Evening: Beryl Stapleton (née Garcia) sends a letter to Sir Henry Baskerville warning him away from the moor. (*HOUN*)

25 September 1889: Selden, the Notting Hill murderer, escapes from Princetown Jail. (*HOUN*)

25 September 1889 – Morning: Sir Henry Baskerville discovers one of his new boots has been stolen during the previous night. (*HOUN*)

25 September 1889 – Morning: Sir Henry Baskerville receives Beryl Stapleton's letter. (*HOUN*)

25 September 1889 – 10 am: James Mortimer arrives at 221b with Sir Henry Baskerville. The mysterious circumstances of Sir Charles Baskerville's death are explained to Henry and plans are made for how to proceed. (*HOUN*)

25 September 1889 – 11:30 am: Sir Henry Baskerville is tailed from 221b by Jack Stapleton in a taxi driven by John Clayton. (*HOUN*)

25 September 1889 – 2 pm: While Watson, Holmes, and James Mortimer are visiting Sir Henry Baskerville in his hotel room, he finds his missing boot and realises a different boot has gone missing. (*HOUN*)

26 September 1889: John Barrymore cleans Sir Charles Baskerville's room and finds the remains of a note from "L.L." in the fireplace. (*HOUN*)

26 September 1889: John and Eliza Barrymore hear that Selden has escaped from Princetown Jail. (*HOUN*)

28 September 1889: Sir Henry Baskerville, James Mortimer, and Watson travel from London to Baskerville Hall. (*HOUN*)

30 September 1889 – Lunch time: Sir Henry Baskerville first meets Beryl Stapleton. (*HOUN*)

10 October 1889: Selden encounters Holmes living secretly on the moor. (*HOUN*)

13 October 1889 – 2 am: Watson witnesses John Barrymore using a candle to signal to Selden. (*HOUN*)

13 October 1889: Watson sends a report to Holmes which, in the text, is titled "First Report of Dr. Watson." (*HOUN*)

15 October 1889 – 2 am: Sir Henry Baskerville and Watson surprise John Barrymore while he is signalling to Selden. Eliza Barrymore explains who John Barrymore has been signalling to and why. Sir Henry Baskerville and Watson attempt to capture Selden but fail. (*HOUN*)

15 October 1889: Sir Henry Baskerville goes off to meet Beryl Stapleton alone. Watson follows and witnesses Jack Stapleton approach them and argue with Sir Henry Baskerville. Later that afternoon Jack Stapleton comes to Baskerville Hall to apologise to Sir Henry and invites them for dinner later in the week. (*HOUN*)

15 October 1889: Watson sends a report to Holmes which, in the text, is titled "Second Report of Dr. Watson." (*HOUN*)

16 October 1889: John Barrymore tells Watson and Sir Henry Baskerville about the note from "L.L." he found in Sir Charles Baskerville's fireplace. (*HOUN*)

17 October 1889: James Mortimer's spaniel wanders onto the moor and is eaten by the Hound. (*HOUN*)

18 October 1889: Frankland wins a legal battle to establish a right of way through the centre of Middleton's park. (*HOUN*)

18 October 1889: Frankland wins a legal battle to close the wood where the Fernworthy folk used to picnic. (*HOUN*)

18 October 1889: Watson travels to Coombe Tracey and interviews Laura Lyons (née Frankland). (*HOUN*)

18 October 1889: Watson visits Frankland on his way back to Baskerville Hall. From here he sees Cartwright delivering food to Holmes. (*HOUN*)

18 October 1889: By following Cartwright, Watson discovers that Holmes has been living secretly on the moor. (*HOUN*)

18 October 1889 – Night: Selden is killed by the Hound (*HOUN*)

19 October 1889 – Morning: Watson and Holmes pretend to return to London. (*HOUN*)

19 October 1889 – 5:40 pm: Watson and Holmes meet Inspector Lestrade at Coombe Tracey train station. (*HOUN*)

19 October 1889 – Evening: Sir Henry Baskerville goes for dinner with the Stapletons at Merripit House. Upon leaving, Jack

Stapleton sets the Hound after him. Holmes kills the Hound and then explains much of what has taken place. (*HOUN*)

October to November 1889: Holmes investigates the atrocious conduct of Colonel Upwood in connection with the famous card scandal of the Nonpareil Club. (*HOUN*)

October to November 1889: Holmes defended the unfortunate Mme. Montpensier from the charge of murder which hung over her in connection with the death of her step-daughter, Mlle. Carere. (*HOUN*)

Late November 1889: Sir Henry Baskerville and James Mortimer visit 221b before setting off on a long voyage to aid Sir Henry Baskerville's recovery from his ordeal. When they have left, Holmes explains the last of the Baskerville case to Watson. (*HOUN*)

January 1890: John Turner dies of diabetes. (*BOSC*)

February 1890: Mary Sutherland meets Hosmer Angel at the Gas-fitters' Ball. Hosmer Angel is her step-father, James Windibank, in disguise. Over the next few weeks, Mary Sutherland falls in love with "Hosmer Angel" and becomes engaged to him. (*IDEN*)

February 1890: *The Sign of Four* is first published publicly. (*SIGN*)

March 1890: Vincent Spaulding starts his apprenticeship with Jabez Wilson. (*REDH*)

During the second week of March 1890: Holmes receives a ring for his services to the reigning family of Holland. (*IDEN*)

14 March 1890: Mary Sutherland is supposed to marry "Hosmer Angel." However, after getting into a cab in his Hosmer Angel disguise, James Windibank gets out the other side and when the cab arrives at the church, it appears that Hosmer Angel has gone missing. (*IDEN*)

15 March 1890: Mary Sutherland places an advertisement in *The Chronicle* seeking Hosmer Angel. (*IDEN*)

17 March 1890: Holmes has ten or twelve cases on hand which present no feature of interest. (*IDEN*)

17 March 1890: Holmes is working on a case referred to him from Marseilles which is an intricate matter. (*IDEN*)

17 March 1890: Mary Sutherland consults Holmes about the disappearance of Hosmer Angel. Holmes asks James Windibank to come to 221b the following evening. (*IDEN*)

18 March 1890 – just after 6 pm: James Windibank arrives at 221b. Holmes reveals that he knows what has happened and threatens James Windibank. Holmes decides not to bother telling Mary Sutherland the truth. (*IDEN*)

20 March 1890: The period of secrecy over the matter of "A Scandal in Bohemia," to which the King of Bohemia swore Holmes and Watson, is over. (*SCAN*)

27 April 1890: The advertisement for the opening in the Red-headed League appears in *The Morning Chronicle*. Vincent Spaulding draws Jabez Wilson's attention to it. They decide to close the shop and go to apply. (*REDH*)

28 April 1890: Jabez Wilson starts his nominal work with the Red-headed League. (*REDH*)

May 1890: Mlle. Carere is found alive and married in New York. (*HOUN*)

02 May 1890: Jabez Wilson receives his first pay from the Red-headed League. (*REDH*)

09 May 1890: Jabez Wilson receives his second pay from the Red-headed League. (*REDH*)

16 May 1890: Jabez Wilson receives his third pay from the Red-headed League. (*REDH*)

23 May 1890: Jabez Wilson receives his fourth pay from the Red-headed League. (*REDH*)

30 May 1890: Jabez Wilson receives his fifth pay from the Red-headed League. (*REDH*)

June 1890: The events of "The Lost Special" take place. Via the papers, Watson has a go at solving the mystery. (*Apocrypha*)

06 June 1890: Jabez Wilson receives his sixth pay from the Red-headed League. (*REDH*)

13 June 1890: Jabez Wilson receives his seventh pay from the Red-headed League. (*REDH*)

20 June 1890: Jabez Wilson receives his eighth pay from the Red-headed League. (*REDH*)

26 June 1890 – Evening: Duncan Ross, Jabez Wilson's senior at the Red-headed League, moves out of the League's offices and leaves a card on the locked door for Jabez Wilson to find. He puts the wrong date on this card—October 9, 1890. Presumably to confuse Jabez Wilson. (*REDH*)

27 June 1890 – 10 am: Jabez Wilson finds the card on the locked door of the office of the Red-headed League announcing that the Red-headed League has been dissolved. After failing to trace Duncan Ross, he consults Holmes. (*REDH*)

27 June 1890 – Morning: After Jabez Wilson leaves, Holmes smokes three pipes over the problem. This takes him fifty minutes. Then they do some investigating at the premises of Jabez Wilson. (*REDH*)

27 June 1890 – Afternoon: Holmes and Watson go to St. James Hall to hear Sarasate play. (*REDH*)

27 June 1890 – 10 pm onwards: In the company of Peter Jones (a Scotland Yard police agent) and Mr. Merryweather (chairman of directors of the City and Suburban Bank), Holmes and Watson go to stake out the vault of the City and Suburban Bank. Eventually they catch Vincent Spaulding breaking in. Holmes explains that he is, in fact, John Clay and what his plan was. (*REDH*)

December 1890 to April 1891: Through the press, Holmes claims to be engaged by the French government on a matter of supreme importance. However, this may have been a lie to throw Moriarty off his track. (*FINA*)

22 December 1890: James Ryder steals the Blue Carbuncle and frames John Horner for the theft. He then goes to his sister, Mrs. Oakshott's, house and hides the gem in the crop of one of her geese. Before he can reclaim it, she sells the geese to Breckenridge, who then immediately sells them to the landlord of the Alpha Inn. (*BLUE*)

22 December 1890 – Evening: John Horner is wrongfully arrested for the theft of the Blue Carbuncle. (*BLUE*)

24 December 1890: Henry Baker spends the evening at the Alpha Inn, collects his goose and in the small hours of the following morning heads home. (*BLUE*)

25 December 1890 – 4 am: Peterson, the commissionaire, witnesses Henry Baker being assaulted by a small knot of roughs and losing his hat and goose. Peterson takes the hat and goose to Holmes later that morning. (*BLUE*)

27 December 1890 – Morning: Holmes returns the goose to Peterson to be cooked and eaten, as it is showing signs of going off. (*BLUE*)

27 December 1890 – Morning: Watson calls upon Holmes and discovers him studying Henry Baker's hat. Peterson arrives, having just found the Blue Carbuncle in the crop of Henry Baker's goose. (*BLUE*)

27 December 1890 – 6:30 pm: Henry Baker, responding to adverts placed by Holmes, comes to 221b to retrieve his hat and collect a replacement goose. In conversation with Holmes, Baker sets him on the trail of where the goose came from. (*BLUE*)

27 December 1890 – Evening: Holmes and Watson capture James Ryder, establish his guilt and let him off. However, they encourage him to run away so that the case against John Horner collapses. (*BLUE*)

Sometime between 22 March 1888 and July 1891: Irene Adler dies. (*SCAN*)

1891: Watson writes up the events of "The Noble Bachelor," but publication is held over until the following year. Possibly due to grief at Holmes's "death." (*NOBL*)

1891: Lord Arthur Saltire is born. (*PRIO*)

January 1891: Holmes starts work in earnest on stopping Moriarty. This includes several long trips to France. This work continues right up to his meeting with Moriarty on 24 April 1891. (*FINA*)

04 January 1891: Holmes crosses the path of Professor James Moriarty. (*FINA*)

23 January 1891: Holmes incommodes Professor James Moriarty. (*FINA*)

15 February 1891: Holmes seriously inconveniences Professor James Moriarty. (*FINA*)

March 1891: Aloysius Garcia and his confederates discover where Don Juan Murillo, The Tiger of San Pedro, is hiding. (*WIST*)

March 1891: Henderson (né Don Juan Murillo, The Tiger of San Pedro) leaves High Gables for what will be a year's absence. (*WIST*)

March 1891: The events of "The Copper Beeches" take place. On day one of the story (a Friday), Violet Hunter first meets Jephro Rucastle. On day four, she consults Holmes. On day five, she goes to the Copper Beeches and the case concludes on day twenty with Holmes exposing the plot against Alice Rucastle. On day twenty-one, Alice Rucastle marries Mr. Fowler. (*COPP*)

30 March 1891 – 9 pm: Colonel Ross's stables at King's Pyland are locked up for the night. John Straker doses Ned Hunter's dinner with opium. A maid, Edith Baxter, takes his dinner out to Ned Hunter, who is on guard at the stables. (*SILV*)

31 March 1891: Holmes absolutely hampers the plans of Professor James Moriarty. (*FINA*)

31 March 1891 – 1 am: John Straker takes Silver Blaze from the stables and leads him out to the moor. He prepares to use a cataract knife to lame Silver Blaze, but Silver Blaze kicks John Straker in the head, killing him. (*SILV*)

31 March 1891 – 7 am: Mrs. Straker notices her husband and Silver Blaze are missing. The alarm is raised, and the body of John Straker is discovered. (*SILV*)

31 March 1891 – Evening: Colonel Ross and Inspector Gregory both telegram Holmes to ask for his help investigating the disappearance of Silver Blaze and the death of John Straker. (*SILV*)

02 April 1891 – 9 am: Holmes asks Watson to accompany him to Tavistock to investigate the disappearance of Silver Blaze and the death of John Straker. (*SILV*)

02 April 1891 – 10 am: Holmes and Watson set off by train for Tavistock. (*SILV*)

02 April 1891 – 6:20 pm: Holmes and Watson arrive at Tavistock and conduct investigations into the disappearance of Silver Blaze and the death of John Straker. Having solved the case to his own satisfaction, Holmes returns to London on the night train with Watson. (*SILV*)

07 April 1891: Silver Blaze wins the Wessex Cup at Winchester and Holmes reveals what took place to Colonel Ross and Watson. (*SILV*)

24 April 1891: Professor James Moriarty finds himself in positive danger of losing his liberty due to continual persecution by Holmes. (*FINA*)

24 April 1891 – Morning: Professor James Moriarty visits Holmes at 221b with the intention of warning Holmes off. (*FINA*)

24 April 1891 – 12 pm: Moriarty has a van try to kill Holmes at the corner of Bentinck Street and Wellbeck Street. (*FINA*)

24 April 1891 – Afternoon: Moriarty has a bricked dropped on Holmes to try to kill him on Vere Street. (*FINA*)

24 April 1891 – Evening: On his way to see Watson, Holmes is attacked by some roughs in the employ of Moriarty. (FINA)

24 April 1891 – Evening: Holmes walks into Watson's consulting room, presents the events of the last few days concerning Professor Moriarty and requests Watson's company on the continent for a week. (FINA)

24 April 1891 – Night: 221b Baker Street is the subject of an arson attack orchestrated by Moriarty. (*FINA*)

25 April 1891: Holmes and Watson set off to Europe together, narrowly escaping the attentions of Professor James Moriarty. They spend the night in Brussels. (*FINA*)

27 April 1891: Holmes's plans are due to come to fruition so that Moriarty and his gang will all be arrested. (*FINA*)

27 April 1891 – Morning: Holmes telegraphs London for news of the case and with Watson leaves Brussels to go to Strasburg. (*FINA*)

27 April 1891 – Afternoon/Evening: In Strasburg, Holmes receives a reply to his telegram of the morning and discovers that Moriarty and a few others have escaped from Holmes's trap. Holmes and Watson set off for Geneva. (*FINA*)

28 April 1891: From Geneva, Holmes and Watson continue a week of travelling through the Valley of the Rhone, Leuk, the Gemini Pass, and Interlaken. (*FINA*)

03 May 1891: Holmes and Watson arrive in Meiringen. (*FINA*)

04 May 1891 – Afternoon: Holmes and Watson set off for the Reichenbach Falls, intending to continue on to Rosenlaui. (*FINA*)

04 May 1891 – Afternoon: After duping Watson into returning to Meiringen, Moriarty confronts Holmes at the Reichenbach Falls. Moriarty is killed. Holmes survives but goes into hiding. (*FINA*)

04 May 1891 – Evening: About three hours after Holmes and Moriarty fight, Watson arrives back at the Reichenbach Falls and convinces himself that Holmes is dead. (*FINA*)

06 May 1891: An account of the death of Sherlock Holmes and Professor James Moriarty is published in the *Journal de Genève*. (*FINA*)

07 May 1891: A Reuter's despatch account of the death of Sherlock Holmes and Professor James Moriarty is published in the English papers. (*FINA*)

11 May 1891: Holmes arrives in Florence. (*EMPT*)

Soon after 11 May 1891: Holmes travels to Tibet in disguise as a Norwegian named Sigerson. (*EMPT*)

Within a few months of May 1891: Watson writes up some account of the events leading up to the "death" of Sherlock Holmes. This is not the full account published as "The Final Problem." Whether and how this earlier account was published is unclear, but Holmes was able to read it during the Great Hiatus. (*EMPT*)

Sometime between 04 May 1891 and 01 April 1894: Inspector Lestrade solves the Molesley Mystery without the aid of Holmes. (*FINA*)

July 1891: "A Scandal in Bohemia" is first published publicly. (*SCAN*)

August 1891: "The Red-Headed League" is first published publicly. (*REDH*)

September 1891: "A Case of Identity" is first published publicly. (*IDEN*)

October 1891: "The Boscombe Valley Mystery" is first published publicly. (*BOSC*)

November 1891: "The Five Orange Pips" is first published publicly. (*FIVE*)

December 1891: "The Man with the Twisted Lip" is first published publicly. (*TWIS*)

1892: Holmes continues his travels in Tibet in disguise as a Norwegian named Sigerson. (*EMPT*)

1892: Robert Ferguson meets and, within a few weeks, marries his second wife, a Peruvian. (*SUSS*)

1892: A crime involving a forged check on the Credit Lyonnais takes place. Holmes was not involved in the case at the time, but later incorrectly suggests that Count Sylvius was involved. (*MAZA*)

January 1892: "The Blue Carbuncle" is first published publicly. (*BLUE*)

February 1892: "The Speckled Band" is first published publicly. (*SPEC*)

13 February 1892: Count Sylvius is involved on a robbery in the train de-luxe to the Riviera. Holmes was not involved in this case at the time. (*MAZA*)

Spring 1892: The events described in "The Man with the Watches" take place. Via the papers, Watson has a go at solving the mystery. (*Apocrypha*)

Early March 1892: Watson suffers a severe bereavement. He struggles to cope. Mycroft, who has been keeping an eye on Watson, begins to worry and wires Holmes to inform him. Holmes carefully stage manages a return, in which Watson and Holmes end up residing together at 221b. It is quite likely that he uses hypnotism to avoid causing a shock to the system of Watson. Through companionship and work, Holmes helps to get Watson back on his feet. (*WIST*)

March 1892: "The Engineer's Thumb" is first published publicly. (*ENGR*)

March 1892: Henderson (né Don Juan Murillo, The Tiger of San Pedro) returns to High Gables after a year's absence. (*WIST*)

March 1892: Holmes and Watson are involved in a case which results in the arrest of Colonel Carruthers. (*WIST*)

19 March 1892: Scott Eccles travels to Esher to spend the night at Wisteria Lodge, the home of Aloysius Garcia. (*WIST*)

19 March 1892 – 11 pm: Scott Eccles retires to bed at Wisteria Lodge. (*WIST*)

19 March 1892 – Night: Aloysius Garcia is murdered by Henderson (né Don Juan Murillo) at High Gable. Henderson realises that Miss Burnett was part of the conspiracy to assassinate him and he places her in captivity. (*WIST*)

20 March 1892 – 1 am: The body of Aloysius Garcia is dumped upon Oxshott Common. (*WIST*)

20 March 1892 – 9 am: Scott Eccles wakes to find Wisteria Lodge abandoned by Aloysius Garcia and his servants. (*WIST*)

20 March 1892 – 1 pm: Unaware that Holmes is supposedly "dead," Scott Eccles sends a telegram to Holmes to request a consultation. (*WIST*)

20 March 1892 – 2:15 pm: Scott Eccles consults Holmes at 221b. (*WIST*)

20 March 1892 – 4 pm: Constable Walters sees the face of the mulatto through the window of Wisteria Lodge. (*WIST*)

20 March 1892 – 6 pm: Holmes, Watson, and Inspector Baynes arrive in Esher to investigate. After an examination of Wisteria Lodge, Holmes and Watson take lodging in Esher. (*WIST*)

23 March 1892 – Late evening: Inspector Baynes arrests the mulatto cook. (*WIST*)

24 March 1892 – Morning: Watson and Holmes learn from the papers that Inspector Baynes has arrested the mulatto cook. (*WIST*)

24 March 1892 – 5 pm: John Warner arrives at Holmes's lodgings to let him know Henderson (né Don Juan Murillo, The Tiger of San Pedro) has made his escape, but that he rescued Miss Burnett before they could get away. Miss Burnett then explains the events to Holmes, Watson, and Inspector Baynes. (*WIST*)

April 1892: Having got Watson back on his feet, Holmes uses hypnosis to make Watson forget the adventure and Holmes's "resurrection" for the time being. (*WIST*)

September 1892: Living under the names Marquess of Montalva and Signor Rulli, Don Juan Murillo and his secretary are murdered in Madrid. (*WIST*)

April 1892: "The Noble Bachelor" is first published publicly. (*NOBL*)

May 1892: "The Beryl Coronet" is first published publicly. (*BERY*)

June 1892: "The Copper Beeches" is first published publicly. (*COPP*)

December 1892: "Silver Blaze" is first published publicly. (*SILV*)

1893: Holmes travels from Tibet to Persia. (*EMPT*)

1893: Holmes travels from Persia to Mecca. (*EMPT*)

1893: Holmes travels from Mecca to Khartoum, where he does some work for the British Foreign Office. (*EMPT*)

1893: Holmes travels from Khartoum to Montpelier, where he studies coal tar derivatives, and makes a trip to Grenoble to have a bust of himself made by Monsieur Oscar Meunier. (*EMPT*)

1893: The British government acquire a monopoly on the Bruce-Partington plans. (*BRUC*)

1893: James Winter (AKA John Garrideb, Killer Evans, and Morecroft) escapes from a U.S. penitentiary and flees to London. (*3GAR*)

January 1893: "The Cardboard Box" is first published publicly. (*CARD*)

February 1893: "The Yellow Face" is first published publicly. (*YELL*)

March 1893: "The Stock-Broker's Clerk" is first published publicly. (*STOC*)

April 1893: "The *Gloria Scott*" is first published publicly. (*GLOR*)

May 1893: "The Musgrave Ritual" is first published publicly. (*MUSG*)

June 1893: "The Reigate Squires" is first published publicly. (*REIG*)

July 1893: "The Crooked Man" is first published publicly. (*CROO*)

August 1893: "The Resident Patient" is first published publicly. (*RESI*)

September 1893: "The Greek Interpreter" is first published publicly. (*GREE*)

October 1893: "The Naval Treaty" is first published publicly. (*NAVA*)

November 1893: Professor Coram decides to hire a secretary. He gets through two others before settling on Mr. Willoughby Smith. (*GOLD*)

November 1893: Letters from Colonel James Moriarty regarding the death and conduct of Sherlock Holmes and Professor James Moriarty appear in the British press which Watson considers incorrect, causing him to write up the matter himself in the form of "The Final Problem." (*FINA*)

December 1893: "The Final Problem" is first published publicly. (*FINA*)

Sometime in 1894 before September: Anna, wife of Professor Coram finishes her penal sentence in Siberia and sets about tracking Professor Coram to recover some important papers. (*GOLD*)

January 1894: The engagement of The Honourable Ronald Adair and Miss Edith Woodley is broken off. (*EMPT*)

30 March 1894 – Between 10 pm and 11:20 pm: The Honourable Ronald Adair is killed. (*EMPT*)

31 March 1894: Still in Montpellier, Holmes is told of the death of Ronald Adair (probably wired by Mycroft Holmes), makes his arrangements and sets off for London. (*EMPT*)

01 April 1894 – 2 pm: Holmes arrives back at 221b Baker Street. (*EMPT*)

01 April 1894 – 6 pm: Investigating the scene of Ronald Adair's murder, Watson visits the scene of the crime. Here he literally bumps into Sherlock Holmes, who is disguised as a bookseller. Watson does not recognise Holmes. (*EMPT*)

01 April 1894 – Evening: Watson returns home. He is soon visited by Holmes, still in his bookseller disguise, who reveals himself and explains most of his actions of the last three years. (*EMPT*)

01 April 1894 – 9:30 pm: Holmes and Watson make their way to Camden House, the empty house opposite 221 Baker Street. (*EMPT*)

02 April 1894 – 12 am: Colonel Sebastian Moran enters Camden House and takes a shot at the bust of Sherlock Holmes. He is arrested by Inspector Lestrade and charged with the murder of Ronald Adair. (*EMPT*)

Sometime between 02 April and 11 August 1894: Holmes and Watson are involved in the case of the papers of Ex-President Murillo. As there were no papers involved in "Wisteria Lodge," it may be assumed that this is a separate case concerning the same villain. (NORW)

Sometime between 02 April and 11 August 1894: Holmes and Watson are involved in the shocking affair of the Dutch steamship *Friesland*, which so nearly cost them both their lives. (*NORW*)

10 August 1894 – 3 pm: Jonas Oldacre arrives at John Hector McFarlane's office and asks him to help arrange his will. He asks McFarlane to come to Oldacre's home that evening to finalise matters. (*NORW*)

10 August 1894 – 9 pm: John Hector McFarlane arrives at Jonas Oldacre's home. They have supper and arrange the legal papers. (*NORW*)

10 August 1894 – 11:30 pm: John Hector McFarlane leaves Jonas Oldacre's home and spends the night at the Anerley Arms, a Norwood hotel. (*NORW*)

10 August 1894 – 11:30 pm: Jonas Oldacre arranges a fire in his own yard is such a way that it appears Jonas Oldacre has been murdered and disposed of. (*NORW*)

11 August 1894 – 12 am: A fire is discovered in the yard of Jonas Oldacre. It has been made to appear that a body has been destroyed in it. (*NORW*)

11 August 1894 – Morning: John Hector McFarlane arrives at 221b, closely followed by Inspector Lestrade. John Hector McFarlane is arrested for the murder of Jonas Oldacre, but is allowed to give his story before being taken away. (*NORW*)

11 August 1894: Holmes spends the day investigating the circumstances of the murder of Jonas Oldacre. (*NORW*)

12 August 1894: Having figured out that Jonas Oldacre faked his own murder, Holmes smokes him out of his hiding place and he is arrested by Lestrade. (*NORW*)

Autumn 1894: Holmes is assisting old Abrahams, who is in mortal terror of his life. (*LADY*)

Autumn 1894: At the request of Miss Dobney, her old governess, Holmes and Watson investigate "The Disappearance of Lady Frances Carfax." The investigation takes several weeks and concludes in London, where Henry "Holy" Peters and Annie Fraser have kidnapped her and are trying to bury her alive. (*LADY*)

Last third of 1894: Holmes and Watson are involved in the repulsive story of the red leech and the terrible death of Crosby the banker. (*GOLD*)

Last third of 1894: Holmes and Watson are involved in the Addleton tragedy and the singular contents of the ancient British barrow. (*GOLD*)

Last third of 1894: Holmes and Watson are involved in the famous Smith-Mortimer succession case. (*GOLD*)

Last third of 1894: Holmes and Watson are involved in the tracking and arrest of Huret, the Boulevard assassin—an exploit which won Holmes an autograph letter of thanks from the French President and the Order of the Legion of Honour. (*GOLD*)

15 November 1894 – between 10:30 am and 11:30 am: Mr. Willoughby Smith returns to Yoxley Old Place after a morning walk. (*GOLD*)

15 November 1894 – between 11 am and 12 pm: Mr. Willoughby Smith is murdered by Anna, wife of Professor Coram. Losing her pince-nez and her way, Anna stumbles into Professor Coram's room and blackmails him into hiding her. (*GOLD*)

15 November 1894 – 3:15 pm: Inspector Stanley Hopkins is assigned to investigate the murder of Mr. Willoughby Smith at Yoxley Old Place. (*GOLD*)

15 November 1894 – 5 pm: Inspector Stanley Hopkins reaches Yoxley Old Place, investigates and returns to London. (*GOLD*)

15 November 1894 – Evening: Inspector Stanley Hopkins arrives at 221b to ask for Holmes's help investigating the murder of Mr. Willoughby Smith at Yoxley Old Place. (*GOLD*)

16 November 1894 – 6 am: Holmes, Watson, and Inspector Stanley Hopkins set off for Yoxley Old Place, arriving around 8 or 9 am. They conduct their investigations. (*GOLD*)

16 November 1894 – 2 pm: Holmes, Watson, and Inspector Stanley Hopkins gather in Professor Coram's room where Holmes reveals where Anna is hiding. Anna then tells them what has happened and why. She then dies as a result of poison she has deliberately consumed. (*GOLD*)

December 1894: An advert appears in *The Times* seeking Violet Smith. Shortly afterwards she meets with Bob Carruthers and Jack Woodley and is presented with their lies about her uncle, Ralph Smith. (*SOLI*)

1895: J. Neil Gibson moves to Thor Place in Hampshire with his wife, Maria Gibson (née Pinto). (*THOR*)

January 1895: James Winter (AKA John Garrideb, Killer Evans, and Morecroft) kills Rodger Prescott in Waterloo Road. (*3GAR*)

March 1895: Charlington Hall, near Carruthers' home, is let out for the summer by Woodley. (*SOLI*)

March 1895: Holmes is in Oxford working on a case involving early English charters. (*3STU*)

15 March 1895 – 3 am: Hilton Soames, in his rooms at St. John's College, Oxford, receives the proofs of the Greek translation papers for the Fortescue Scholarship examinations. (*3STU*)

15 March 1895 – 4:30 pm: Hilton Soames takes a break from checking examination proofs and spends rather more than an hour taking tea in a friend's rooms. (*3STU*)

15 March 1895 – 5:40 pm: Hilton Soames returns to his rooms to discover that someone has rummaged his papers to cheat in the Greek translation examination. There is a brief examination of the room and a discussion with Bannister. (*3STU*)

15 March 1895 – 5:45 pm: Hilton Soames sets off to Holmes's lodgings near the Bodleian Library to request Holmes's help. (*3STU*)

15 March 1895 – 5:54 pm: Hilton Soames arrives at Holmes's lodgings. (*3STU*)

15 March 1895 – 6:03 pm: Holmes, Watson, and Hilton Soames set off for Hilton Soames's rooms. (*3STU*)

15 March 1895 – 6:12 pm: Holmes, Watson, and Hilton Soames arrive back at Hilton Soames's rooms. (*3STU*)

15 March 1895 – 9 pm: Holmes and Watson return to their lodgings. (*3STU*)

16 March 1895: The first day of the examination for the Fortescue Scholarship. (*3STU*)

16 March 1895 – Early morning: After a sleepless night of feeling guilty, Gilchrist writes a letter to Hilton Soames, withdrawing from the Fortescue Scholarship examinations. (*3STU*)

16 March 1895 – 6 am: Holmes conducts some investigations into Hilton Soames's problem. (*3STU*)

16 March 1895 – 8 am: Holmes wakes Watson, they return to Hilton Soames's rooms and Holmes reveals all. Gilchrist withdraws from the scholarship examination so that it may proceed as planned. (*3STU*)

13 April 1895: Violet Smith is first followed to the train station by Carruthers in disguise. (*SOLI*)

15 April 1895: Violet Smith is followed back from the train station by Carruthers in disguise. (*SOLI*)

20 April 1895: Violet Smith is followed to the train station by Carruthers in disguise. (*SOLI*)

22 April 1895: Violet Smith is followed back from the train station by Carruthers in disguise. (*SOLI*)

23 April 1895: Holmes receives a letter from Violet Smith announcing her intention to visit and consult Holmes the following Saturday. (*SOLI*)

27 April 1895: Holmes is working on a very abstruse and complicated problem concerning the peculiar persecution to which John Vincent Harden, the well-known tobacco millionaire, had been subjected. (*SOLI*)

27 April 1895 – Just before noon: Violet Smith is followed to the train station by Carruthers in disguise. (*SOLI*)

27 April 1895: Violet Smith visits Holmes to present her case. (*SOLI*)

29 April 1895 – 9:13 am: Watson heads to Farnham ahead of Violet Smith. (*SOLI*)

29 April 1895: Watson witnesses Violet Smith being followed back from the train station by Carruthers in disguise. (*SOLI*)

30 April 1895: Violet Smith sends a note to Holmes informing him she had been followed again on the 29th. (*SOLI*)

30 April 1895: Holmes goes to Farnham to investigate and gets into a fight with Woodley. (*SOLI*)

02 May 1895: Woodley receives a telegram informing him that Ralph Smith has died. He shares this information with Carruthers. (*SOLI*)

02 May 1895: Violet Smith sends Holmes a note saying she intends to leave Farnham permanently on 04 May 1895 because Carruthers has proposed to her. (*SOLI*)

04 May 1895: Violet Smith is abducted on her way to the train station and Woodley uses ex-clergyman Williamson to try to force Violet Smith to marry him. Holmes, Watson, and Carruthers manage to rescue her and arrest Woodley and Williamson. (*SOLI*)

Early June 1895: Mary Fraser and her maid, Theresa Wright, leave Australia to come to England on the *Rock of Gibraltar* steam ship. (*ABBE*)

June 1895: Jack Croker meets Mary Fraser and her maid, Theresa Wright, aboard the *Rock of Gibraltar* steam ship. He falls in love with Mary Fraser. (*ABBE*)

June 1895: Holmes investigates the sudden death of Cardinal Tosca at the express desire of His Holiness the Pope. (*BLAC*)

June 1895: Holmes catches Wilson, the notorious canary-trainer, which removes a plague-spot from the East-End of London. (*BLAC*)

Late June 1895: Mary Fraser and her maid, Theresa Wright, arrive in England. (*ABBE*)

Early July 1895: Mary Fraser and her maid, Theresa Wright, meet Sir Eustace Brackenstall for the first time. (*ABBE*)

01 July 1895: Through the window of the cabin at Woodman's Lee, Mr. Slater sees "Black" Peter Carey in conversation with Patrick Cairns. Patrick Cairns has found "Black" Peter Carey and is attempting to blackmail him over the murder of Mr. Neligan in 1883. (*BLAC*)

03 July 1895 – 2 am: "Black" Peter Carey attacks and is killed by Patrick Cairns at Woodman's Lee in Sussex. (*BLAC*)

03 July 1895: John Hopley Neligan arrives at Bramblebyre Hotel near Woodman's Lee. (*BLAC*)

03 July 1895 – 12 pm: The body of "Black" Peter Carey is discovered. (*BLAC*)

03 July 1895 – 1 pm: Inspector Stanley Hopkins arrives at Woodman's Lee to investigate the murder of "Black" Peter Carey. (*BLAC*)

04 to 09 July 1895: Holmes is absent from 221b for many long periods investigating the murder of "Black" Peter Carey. (*BLAC*)

09 July 1895: John Hopley Neligan attempts and fails to break into "Black" Peter Carey's cabin. (*BLAC*)

10 July 1895 – Early morning: Holmes experiments with a spear, attempting to skewer a pig at Allardyce's butcher shop. (*BLAC*)

10 July 1895: Inspector Stanley Hopkins arrives at 221b to ask for Holmes's help investigating the murder of "Black" Peter Carey. Holmes, Watson and Inspector Stanley Hopkins all travel to Woodman's Lee. (*BLAC*)

10 July 1895 – 11 pm: Holmes, Watson, and Inspector Stanley Hopkins set up an ambush at Woodman's Lee. (*BLAC*)

11 July 1895 – 2:30 am: Holmes, Watson, and Inspector Stanley Hopkins catch John Hopley Neligan in their ambush at Woodman's Lee. John Hopley Neligan tells them the story of his father's disappearance and the connection with "Black" Peter Carey. (*BLAC*)

12 July 1895 – 9:30 am: Patrick Cairns is arrested at 221b for the murder of "Black" Peter Carey. He gives his account of what happened on the *Sea Unicorn* in 1883. (*BLAC*)

11 November 1895: Cadogan West first becomes concerned about the security of the Bruce-Partington Plans. (*BRUC*)

18 November 1895: Hugo Oberstein is known to be in London. (*BRUC*)

18 November 1895: Holmes spends the day at 221b cross-indexing his reference books. (*BRUC*)

18 November 1895 – 3 pm: Sir James Walter leaves Woolwich Arsenal to go to Admiral Sinclair's house in Barclay Square. (*BRUC*)

18 November 1895 – 5 pm: The offices at the Woolwich Arsenal close. (*BRUC*)

18 November 1895 – 7:30 pm: While out with his fiancée, Violet Westbury, Cadogan West suddenly abandons her to follow Colonel Walter Valentine. (*BRUC*)

18 November 1895 – 8:15 pm: Cadogan West takes a train from Woolwich Station into London. (*BRUC*)

18 November 1895 – 11:40 pm: The body of Cadogan West falls from the top of a train onto the tracks near Aldgate Station. (*BRUC*)

19 November 1895 – 6 am: The body of Cadogan West is found near Aldgate Station on the Underground. (*BRUC*)

19 November 1895: Holmes spends the day researching and writing about the polyphonic motets of Lassus. (*BRUC*)

19 November 1895 – 12 pm: Violet Westbury is informed of the death of Cadogan West. (*BRUC*)

20 November 1895: Holmes spends the day researching and writing about the polyphonic motets of Lassus. (*BRUC*)

21 November 1895: Hugo Oberstein is known to have left London. (*BRUC*)

21 November 1895 – Morning: Sir James Walter dies due to his shock at the Bruce-Partington Plans being stolen. (*BRUC*)

21 November 1895: Mycroft Holmes comes to 221b to ask Sherlock Holmes to investigate the death of Cadogan West and the theft of the Bruce-Partington Plans. (*BRUC*)

22 November 1895 – After breakfast: Mycroft Holmes and Inspector Lestrade meet Sherlock Holmes at 221b. Holmes updates them on his progress and they make plans for an ambush that evening. (*BRUC*)

22 November 1895: Holmes spends some of the day researching and writing about the polyphonic motets of Lassus. (*BRUC*)

22 November 1895 – 9 pm: Sherlock Holmes, Watson, Mycroft Holmes, and Inspector Lestrade set up their ambush at Caulfield Gardens. (*BRUC*)

22 November 1895 – 11 pm: Sherlock Holmes, Watson, Mycroft Holmes, and Inspector Lestrade capture Colonel Valentine Walter in their ambush. Colonel Valentine Walter is arrested for the theft of the Bruce-Partington Plans and tells all. (*BRUC*)

23 November 1895 – 12 pm: Hugo Oberstein is tricked into a meeting at the Charing Cross Hotel and is arrested for the murder of Cadogan West and the theft of the Bruce-Partington Plans. (*BRUC*)

December 1895: Holmes spends a day at Windsor, where he receives an emerald tie-pin from Queen Victoria. (*BRUC*)

End of summer 1895: Violet Smith is due to marry Cyril Morton. (*SOLI*)

1896: Josiah Amberley retires and moves to a house called The Haven in Lewisham. (*RETI*)

1896: In secret, Godfrey Staunton marries Mrs. Staunton. (*MISS*)

January 1896: Mary Fraser marries Sir Eustace Brackenstall and becomes Lady Mary Brackenstall. (*ABBE*)

At some point between September and December 1896: A month after Leonardo the Strongman drowns, Mrs. Ronder is suffering mentally. She agrees to let Mrs. Merrilow, her landlady, bring Holmes in to take her confession. Mrs. Ronder tells all to Holmes, revealing the true events of the Abbas Parva Tragedy. Holmes tries to talk her out of suicide. Two days later Mrs. Ronder sends her poison to Holmes to indicate that she has decided not to kill herself. (*VEIL*)

Early November 1896: The conversation described in "The Field Bazaar" takes place. (*Apocrypha*)

November 1896: Captain Jack Croker waits for his next voyage at his family home in Sydenham. He runs into Theresa Wright and through her, begins visiting Lady Mary Brackenstall (née Fraser) in secret. (*ABBE*)

20 November 1896: "The Field Bazaar" is first published publicly. (*Apocrypha*)

1897: Colonel Walter Valentine dies in prison. (*BRUC*)

Early 1897: Josiah Amberley marries Mrs. Amberley. (*RETI*)

Early 1897: Robert Ferguson's second son is born by his second wife. (*SUSS*)

04 January 1897: The Lewisham gang of burglars, the three Randalls, burgle a house in Sydenham. (*ABBE*)

17 January 1897 – Late evening: At Abbey Grange, Captain Jack Croker visits Lady Mary Brackenstall in secret. They are discovered by Sir Eustace Brackenstall and in the ensuing argument, Jack Croker kills Eustace Brackenstall. Jack Croker, Mary Brackenstall, and Mary's maid, Theresa Wright, arrange things to look like it was a burglary gone wrong, Jack Croker flees the scene and the police are called. (*ABBE*)

18 January 1897 – 3:30 am: Inspector Stanley Hopkins sends a note to Holmes asking for his assistance at Abbey Grange. (*ABBE*)

18 January 1897 – Early morning: Holmes receives Inspector Stanley Hopkins's note, wakes Watson and they both set off for Abbey Grange. (*ABBE*)

18 January 1897 – Morning: Holmes and Watson arrive at Abbey Grange, make some investigations and then head back to London. They do not get far before they return to Abbey Grange and conduct further investigations. These completed, they return to London. (*ABBE*)

18 January 1897 – Morning: The Lewisham gang of burglars, the three Randalls, are arrested in New York. (*ABBE*)

18 January 1897 – Evening: Captain Jack Croker is summoned to 221b, where he is forced to tell Holmes and Watson what happened. They decide not to tell the police and let Jack Croker get away. He plans to return in a year to continue his relationship with Lady Mary Brackenstall (née Fraser). (*ABBE*)

20 January 1897: Captain Jack Croker leaves England on the *Bass Rock*. (*ABBE*)

March 1897: Holmes's iron constitution shows some signs of giving way. Dr. Moore Agar advises Holmes that he requires complete rest. As a result, Watson accompanies Holmes on a holiday in Cornwall. (*DEVI*)

01 March 1897: Mortimer Tregennis visits Dr. Leon Sterndale, is shown the devil's foot root powder, and endeavours to steal some before he leaves. (*DEVI*)

15 March 1897 – 10:15 pm: Having spent an evening playing cards with his siblings (Owen, George, and Brenda) at their home, Mortimer Tregennis slips some powdered devil's foot root into the fire and leaves for his home at the vicarage. Brenda dies and Owen and George are sent insane. (*DEVI*)

16 March 1897 – Morning: Mortimer Tregennis and Reverend Roundhay arrive at Poldhu Cottage, the holiday home of Holmes and Watson, to request his help investigating the attack on Mortimer Tregennis's brothers and sister. (*DEVI*)

16 March 1897: Dr. Leon Sterndale sets off to return to Africa. However, he is intercepted at Plymouth by a telegram from the Reverend Roundhay telling him Brenda Tregennis is dead. He returns to Cornwall to exact his revenge. (*DEVI*)

16 March 1897: After investigating the attack at the Tregennis house, Watson and Holmes encounter Dr. Leon Sterndale at Poldhu Cottage. Following a brief conversation, Holmes abandons Watson to follow Dr. Leon Sterndale for a while. (*DEVI*)

17 March 1897 – 6:30 am: Dr. Leon Sterndale visits Mortimer Tregennis at the vicarage. He forces Mortimer Tregennis to inhale the fumes of devil's foot root and Mortimer Tregennis dies. (*DEVI*)

17 March 1897 – Morning: Reverend Roundhay returns to Poldhu Cottage to inform Holmes and Watson that Mortimer Tregennis had died in the night in similar circumstances to his siblings. Holmes and Watson go with Reverend Roundhay to the vicarage to examine the scene. Holmes finds some unburnt powdered devil's foot root on the lamp in Mortimer Tregennis's room. He takes some of it. (*DEVI*)

18 March 1897: Holmes summons Dr. Leon Sterndale to Poldhu Cottage. (*DEVI*)

18 March 1897 – Afternoon: Holmes and Watson experiment with the powdered devil's foot root, almost killing themselves in the process. (*DEVI*)

18 March 1897: Dr. Leon Sterndale arrives at Poldhu Cottage and after some conversation he explains all. Holmes decides not to tell the police and advises Dr. Leon Sterndale to bury himself in his work in Africa. (*DEVI*)

June 1897: Hilton Cubitt comes to London for a month to celebrate the Diamond Jubilee. During this time, he meets Elsie Patrick and they marry before returning to Ridling Thorpe Manor, Norfolk. (*DANC*)

22 June 1897: Queen Victoria's Diamond Jubilee. (*DANC*)

July 1897: Nathan Garrideb moves into rooms which were previously occupied by forger Rodger Prescott. (*3GAR*)

July 1897: Jack Ferguson tests out his stepmother's poison darts on the family dog, Carlo. (*SUSS*)

Around 19 October 1897: Jack Ferguson fires a poison dart at his infant half-brother. The baby is saved when the baby's mother sucks out the poison. However, the baby's nurse, Mrs. Mason, witnesses this and believes the mother has attacked the baby. (*SUSS*)

18 November 1897: Mrs. Mason decides to tell Robert Ferguson about the attack she believes she witnessed by his wife on their son the month before. As this is taking place, Jack Ferguson tries to murder his half-brother again. Mrs. Ferguson sucks out the poison again. Robert Ferguson and the nurse walk in to discover this and draw the wrong conclusions again. Appalled at the accusations, Mrs. Ferguson takes to her bed with a brain fever. (*SUSS*)

19 November 1897: Robert Ferguson consults the firm of Morrison, Morrison, and Dodd regarding his wife and her apparent vampiric nature. They advise him to contact Holmes. (*SUSS*)

19 November 1897: The firm of Morrison, Morrison, and Dodd send a letter to Holmes informing him they have advised Robert Ferguson to consult Holmes on the matter of vampires. Holmes receives this letter the same day. (*SUSS*)

19 November 1897: Holmes receives a letter from Robert Ferguson outlining his problem and asking to be allowed to consult Holmes. In it, he attempts, unsuccessfully, to pretend he is acting on behalf of a friend. (*SUSS*)

20 November 1897 – 10 am: Robert Ferguson arrives at 221b and consults Holmes about his apparently vampiric wife. (*SUSS*)

20 November 1897 – 2 pm: Holmes and Watson set off for Sussex to investigate Robert Ferguson's problems. They arrive in the evening. (*SUSS*)

20 November 1897 – Evening: Holmes quickly solves Robert Ferguson's case and reveals all. (*SUSS*)

21 November 1897: Holmes messages the firm of Morrison, Morrison, and Dodd to say that he has dealt with Robert Ferguson's case. (*SUSS*)

December 1897: Dr. Leslie Armstrong diagnoses Mrs. Staunton with terminal consumption. (*MISS*)

12 December 1897: Cyril Overton brings the Cambridge team to London for the Varsity Match. (*MISS*)

12 December 1897 – 6 pm: Godfrey Staunton receives a telegram from Dr. Leslie Armstrong regarding his wife's health. He replies, asking Dr. Armstrong to continue to stand by them. (*MISS*)

12 December 1897 – 10:30 pm: Godfrey Staunton receives a message regarding the worsening health of his secret wife. He immediately leaves to return to Cambridge to see her. (*MISS*)

13 December 1897 – Morning: Cyril Overton discovers Godfrey Staunton is missing. (*MISS*)

13 December 1897 – 10:36 am: Cyril Overton sends a telegram to Holmes announcing his intention to consult him the same day. Soon after, he arrives at 221b and asks for Holmes's help locating Godfrey Staunton. Holmes and Watson examine Godfrey Staunton's room and travel to Cambridge to investigate. (*MISS*)

13 December 1897 – Evening: Holmes and Watson speak to Dr. Leslie Armstrong. Assuming they are working for Godfrey's uncle (Lord Mount-James), Dr. Armstrong refuses to help. (*MISS*)

13 December 1897 – 6:30 pm: Holmes tries to follow Dr. Leslie Armstrong's carriage on a bicycle, but is caught and warned off. (*MISS*)

14 December 1897: Holmes and Watson fruitlessly investigate the disappearance of Godfrey Staunton in Cambridge. (*MISS*)

14 December 1897: The Varsity Match between Cambridge and Oxford takes place without Godfrey Staunton. Oxford win. (*MISS*)

15 December 1897: Holmes and Watson use a tracker dog to follow Dr. Leslie Armstrong and discover the house Godfrey Staunton has been hiding in. Staunton is at the side of his wife, who has just died of consumption. (*MISS*)

1898: Gennaro and Emilia Lucca elope from Italy to New York. (*REDC*)

1898: "The Lost Special" is first published publicly. (*Apocrypha*)

1898: "The Man with the Watches" is first published publicly. (*Apocrypha*)

January 1898: Captain Jack Croker intends to return to Lady Mary Brackenstall (née Fraser) to resume their relationship. (*ABBE*)

Late June 1898: Elsie Cubitt receives a letter from Abe Slaney which causes her distress. She burns it without showing it to her husband. (*DANC*)

21 June 1898: Hilton Cubitt finds an example of the dancing men cipher in chalk on one of his window sills. (*DANC*)

29 June 1898: Thurston asks Watson to go in with him on some South African property. (*DANC*)

26 July 1898 – Morning: Hilton Cubitt finds an example of the dancing men cipher on paper left on his sundial. (*DANC*)

26 July 1898 – Evening: Watson spends the evening playing billiards with Thurston at their club. (*DANC*)

27 July 1898 – Morning: Hilton Cubitt calls on Holmes at 221b seeking advice regarding the images of dancing men and the effect they are having on his wife. Holmes asks him to make a note of any more that appear and when there are fresh developments, to call Holmes in again. (*DANC*)

28 July 1898: Hilton Cubitt finds another example of the dancing men cipher in chalk on the door of the tool-house. (*DANC*)

30 July 1898: Hilton Cubitt finds another example of the dancing men cipher in chalk on the door of the tool-house. (*DANC*)

02 August 1898: Hilton Cubitt finds another example of the dancing men cipher on paper left on his sundial. (*DANC*)

03 August 1898: Hilton Cubitt finds another example of the dancing men cipher in chalk on the door of the tool-house. (*DANC*)

10 August 1898 – Afternoon: Hilton Cubitt returns to 221b to present his new evidence. He then returns to Ridling Thorpe Manor to be with his wife. Holmes then sets about cracking the dancing men cipher, does so and best part solves the case. (*DANC*)

12 August 1898 – Morning: Hilton Cubitt finds a long example of the dancing men cipher on the sundial. (*DANC*)

12 August 1898 – Evening: Holmes receives a telegram from Hilton Cubitt saying that he had found another example of the dancing men cipher. (*DANC*)

13 August 1898 – 3 am: Elsie Cubitt meets Abe Slaney at a window of Ridling Thorpe Manor. She tries to get him to leave her alone. Hilton Cubitt enters, and shots are fired by both Hilton Cubitt and Abe Slaney. Hilton Cubitt is killed. Elsie Cubitt is shot in the head but survives. Abe Slaney escapes. (*DANC*)

13 August 1898 – 4 am: Inspector Martin and a constable arrive at Ridling Thorpe Manor. (*DANC*)

13 August 1898 – Morning: Holmes and Watson arrive at Ridling Thorpe Manor and discover the tragedy of the night before. Holmes uses the cipher to send for Abe Slaney, making him believe Elsie Cubitt sent the message. Holmes explains how he cracked the cipher. Abe Slaney arrives and is arrested. All is revealed. (*DANC*)

20 May 1899: Beppo receives his last pay from Gelder & Co. (*SIXN*)

Within the week after 20 May 1899: The black pearl of the Borgias is stolen. Two days later, Beppo hides it in a cast of Napoleon and is arrested for attacking another Italian in the street. (*SIXN*)

28 May 1899: Believing they are having an affair, Josiah Amberley murders his wife and Ray Ernest. He then endeavours to make it look as if they have run away. (*RETI*)

03 June 1899: Gelder & Co sell the six casts of Napoleon, one of which contains the black pearl of the Borgias. (*SIXN*)

04 June 1899: Holmes is engaged in the case of the two Coptic Patriarchs. (*RETI*)

04 June 1899 – Morning: As part of his ruse to pretend his wife has run away, Josiah Amberley consults Holmes. As he returns home to 221b, Watson passes Josiah Amberley leaving. (*RETI*)

04 June 1899 – Afternoon: Watson conducts an ineffective investigation at Josiah Amberley's home in Lewisham. (*RETI*)

05 June 1899: Holmes tricks Josiah Amberley into going away for the night with Watson to keep a watch on him. Holmes conducts real investigations at The Haven, Josiah Amberley's home. He bumps into another detective, Mr. Barker, and between them they solve the case. (*RETI*)

06 June 1899: When Watson and Josiah Amberley return, Holmes and Mr. Barker capture Josiah Amberley, explain all and have him arrested. (*RETI*)

08 June 1899: An inaccurate account of the crimes of Josiah Amberley appears in the *North Surrey Observer*. (*RETI*)

11 October 1899: The Boer War breaks out. (*History*)

1900: Shinwell "Porky" Johnson first begins to act as an agent for Holmes. (*ILLU*)

1900: The Duke of Holdernesse becomes Lord Lieutenant of Hallamshire. (*PRIO*)

June 1900: Holmes is working on the Conk-Singleton forgery case. (*SIXN*)

June 1900: At the request of Lestrade, Holmes, and Watson investigate the events of the "Six Napoleons," eventually solving the case, capturing Beppo and locating the black pearl of the Borgias. (*SIXN*)

01 October 1900 – 5 pm: J. Neil Gibson returns from town to Thor Place manor house and remains there for the rest of the evening. (*THOR*)

01 October 1900 – 8:30 pm: The residents of Thor Place manor house have dinner. (*THOR*)

01 October 1900 – 9 pm: As they had arranged, Grace Dunbar meets with Maria Gibson on Thor Bridge. After some heated conversation, Grace Dunbar leaves Maria Gibson on the bridge and returns to the manor house. (*THOR*)

01 October 1900 – A while after 9 pm: Maria Gibson commits suicide in an intricate way designed to make it seem that Grace Dunbar murdered her. (*THOR*)

02 October 1900 – 11 am: The body of Maria Gibson is discovered by a gamekeeper on the Thor Place estate. (*THOR*)

02 October 1900: Grace Dunbar is arrested for the murder of Maria Gibson. (*THOR*)

03 October 1900: J. Neil Gibson sends a letter to Holmes asking for his help clearing Grace Dunbar of the murder of his wife and saying that he will call upon Holmes at 11 am the following day. (*THOR*)

04 October 1900 – Morning: Holmes receives the letter from J. Neil Gibson and shares it with Watson. Holmes fills Watson in on the details of the case and they receive a brief visit from J. Neil Gibson's estate manager, Marlow Bates, warning them that Neil Gibson is a villainous character. (*THOR*)

04 October 1900 – 11 am: J. Neil Gibson arrives at 221b. There is some heated conversation and for a while Gibson leaves 221b. Eventually, however, the full case is laid before Holmes and Watson and they all travel to Thor Place, Hampshire. (*THOR*)

05 October 1900 – Morning: Holmes speaks to Grace Dunbar who is jailed in Winchester. (*THOR*)

05 October 1900 – 5:30 pm: Holmes, having solved the case, gives a demonstration of what happened on Thor Bridge to Sergeant Coventry and Watson. (*THOR*)

05 October 1900 – Evening: At their Inn where they are spending the night, Holmes gives Watson a full account of what actually happened. (*THOR*)

06 October 1900 – Morning: Holmes meets with J. Neil Gibson and steps are taken for the vindication of Grace Dunbar. (*THOR*)

1901: Baron Adelbert Gruner breaks off an affair with Kitty Winter. (*ILLU*)

1901: James Winter (AKA John Garrideb, Killer Evans, and Morecroft) is released from prison. (*3GAR*)

1901: Holmes assists Mr. Fairdale Hobbs, one of Mrs. Warren's lodgers, in a simple matter. (*REDC*)

January 1901: James M. Dodd and Godfrey Emsworth join the Middlesex Corps of the Imperial Yeomanry. (*BLAN*)

22 January 1901: Queen Victoria dies. (*History*)

April 1901: The Duke and Duchess of Holdernesse separate. This is due to tensions caused by the Duke's illegitimate son, James Wilder. The Duchess moves to the South of France. (*PRIO*)

01 May 1901: Lord Arthur Saltire arrives at the Priory School. (*PRIO*)

12 May 1901: The Duke of Holdernesse writes a letter to Lord Arthur Saltire, but before it is sent James Wilder tampers with it, making it seem that if Arthur runs away on the night of 13 May 1901, he will be reunited with his mother. (*PRIO*)

13 May 1901 – Morning: Lord Arthur Saltire receives the letter he believes is from his mother. (*PRIO*)

13 May 1901 – Night: Lord Arthur Saltire is last seen at the Priory School. (*PRIO*)

14 May 1901 – 12 am: Lord Arthur Saltire runs away from the school only to be abducted by James Wilder and Reuben Hayes. Heidegger, the German master, sees Lord Arthur Saltire running away and sets after him. When he catches up, Reuben Hayes murders him. Lord Arthur Saltire is taken to Reuben Hayes' inn, The Fighting Cock, where he is held prisoner. (*PRIO*)

14 May 1901 – 7 am: It is discovered that Lord Arthur Saltire and Heidegger, the German master, are missing. (*PRIO*)

14 May 1901: Some gipsies (sic) who were camped on moorland near the Priory School move on. (*PRIO*)

15 May 1901 – Evening: A rumour about the disappearance of Lord Arthur Saltire appears in *The Globe*. (*PRIO*)

16 May 1901 – Morning: Dr. Thorneycroft Huxtable arrives at 221b to consult Holmes about the disappearance of Lord Arthur Saltire. (*PRIO*)

16 May 1901 – Evening: Holmes, Watson, and Dr. Thorneycroft Huxtable travel to Hallamshire to investigate the disappearance of Lord Arthur Saltire. (*PRIO*)

17 May 1901: Holmes and Watson continue their investigations in Hallamshire. They discover the body of Heidegger, the German master. (*PRIO*)

17 May 1901: The Duke of Holdernesse and James Wilder learn that Reuben Hayes murdered Heidegger. James Wilder is so horrified he tells his father, the Duke, everything. The Duke tries to help James Wilder cover everything up and visits his legitimate son, Lord Arthur Saltire, at The Fighting Cock. (*PRIO*)

17 May 1901 – 11 pm: At Holmes's direction, Reuben Hayes is arrested for his part in the abduction of Lord Arthur Saltire and the murder of Heidegger, the German master. (*PRIO*)

18 May 1901 – Morning: The Duke of Holdernesse banishes his first son, James Wilder, to Australia and writes to the Duchess of Holdernesse with a view to reconciliation. (*PRIO*)

18 May 1901 – 11:30 am: Holmes and Watson meet with the Duke of Holdernesse. Holmes reveals that he knows all and as good as blackmails the Duke for six thousand pounds. A carriage is then sent to The Fighting Cock to rescue Lord Arthur Saltire. (*PRIO*)

August 1901: *The Hound of the Baskervilles* is first published publicly. (*HOUN*)

1902: Ex-clergyman Williamson is due to be released from prison. (*SOLI*)

January 1902 – Morning: During Boer War combat at Buffelsspruit, Pretoria, Godfrey Emsworth is shot. (*BLAN*)

January 1902 – Evening: Having been shot, Godfrey Emsworth is carried away by his horse. He regains consciousness that evening and finds himself in a hospice for lepers where he remains for about a week. (*BLAN*)

January 1902: Godfrey Emsworth is moved to a hospital in Cape Town, where he writes a letter to James M. Dodd. (*BLAN*)

31 May 1902: The conclusion of the Boer War. (*History*)

Spring 1902: Steve Dixie and Barney Stockdale are involved in the killing of young Perkins outside the Holborn Bar. While Holmes does not deal with the case directly, he does take an interest. (*3GAB*)

Summer 1902: The main events of "The Three Gables" take place. Holmes is engaged by Mrs. Mary Maberley to look into peculiar goings on at The Three Gables. That night she is burgled. Holmes solves the mystery and secretly gets compensation for Mrs. Mary Maberley from Isadora Klein. (*3GAB*)

June 1902: Holmes refuses a knighthood for services which we are not told about. (*3GAR*)

24 June 1902: James Winter, pretending to be John Garrideb, meets Nathan Garrideb to tell him lies about needing to find a third Garrideb. (*3GAR*)

26 June 1902 – Morning: Holmes receives a letter from Nathan Garrideb requesting his help locating a third Garrideb. (*3GAR*)

26 June 1902 – Morning: "John Garrideb" visits Nathan Garrideb at his home and discovers that Nathan Garrideb has contacted Holmes. (*3GAR*)

26 June 1902 – Morning: James Winter, pretending to be John Garrideb, arrives at 221b to discourage Holmes from looking into the business of the three Garridebs. (*3GAR*)

26 June 1902 – Evening: Holmes and Watson visit Nathan Garrideb in his rooms to gather information. "John Garrideb" arrives at the rooms and announces he has located a third Garrideb in Birmingham and that Nathan Garrideb must leave at 12 pm and travel to meet him the following day at 4 pm. (*3GAR*)

27 June 1902 – 4 pm: With Nathan Garrideb away, Holmes and Watson stake out his rooms and catch James Winter (AKA John Garrideb, Killer Evans, and Morecroft) in the act of retrieving hidden money forged by Rodger Prescott. (*3GAR*)

July 1902: Godfrey Emsworth is in a Netley Hospital in Southampton where he writes a letter to James M. Dodd. From there he returns home to Tuxbury Old Park. He develops signs of skin disease. His parents keep him hidden because they believe he has contracted leprosy. (*BLAN*)

August 1902: Gennaro and Emilia Lucca encounter Giuseppe Gorgiano and his gang in New York. Eventually Gennaro and Emilia are forced to flee to London. (*REDC*)

09 August 1902: Coronation of King Edward VII. (*History*)

02 September 1902: Sir James Damery sends Holmes a note to say he will visit 221b the following evening. (*ILLU*)

03 September 1902: Holmes and Watson visit a Turkish bath together. (*ILLU*)

03 September 1902 – 4:30 pm: Sir James Damery meets Watson and Holmes at 221b where he requests Holmes's help breaking off the engagement of Violet de Merville and Baron Adelbert Gruner. Holmes accepts and begins work by enlisting the help of Shinwell "Porky" Johnson and speaking with Baron Adelbert Gruner. (*ILLU*)

04 September 1902 – 5:30 pm: Holmes, Watson, and Kitty Winter visit Violet de Merville to explain what a bad person Baron Adelbert Gruner is. Violet de Merville refuses to take heed. (*ILLU*)

06 September 1902 – just before 12 pm: Outside the Cafe Royal in Regent Street, Holmes is attacked by two thugs hired by Baron Adelbert Gruner. His wounds require stitches. (*ILLU*)

06 September 1902 – Evening: Watson learns through newspaper headlines that Holmes has been attacked. (*ILLU*)

14 September 1902: Holmes has his stitches from the attack on 06 September 1902 removed. (*ILLU*)

14 September 1902 – Evening: Watson begins a session of studying Chinese pottery which takes him into the afternoon of 15 September 1902. (*ILLU*)

14 September 1902: Having fled New York a few days ago, Gennaro Lucca takes lodgings with Mrs. Warren. That evening he secretly swaps places with his wife, Emilia Lucca, who will stay hidden in the room for the next eleven days. (*REDC*)

15 September 1902 – Evening: Holmes, Watson, and Kitty Winter visit the home of Baron Adelbert Gruner. While Watson distracts Baron Adelbert Gruner, Holmes breaks in and steals his lust diary. Baron Adelbert Gruner realises what is happening and pursues Holmes. The baron is stopped when Kitty Winter unexpectedly throws vitriol in his face. (*ILLU*)

15 September 1902 – Late Evening: Watson arrives back at 221b where he meets up with Holmes. Sir James Damery arrives, and they give him Baron Adelbert Gruner's lust diary to use to demonstrate to Violet de Merville what sort of a man the Baron is. (*ILLU*)

16 September 1902: Gennaro Lucca sends his first secret message to Emilia Lucca via the agony columns of the *Daily Gazette*. (*REDC*)

18 September 1902: An article appears in the *Morning Post* to say that the marriage of Violet de Merville and Baron Adelbert Gruner has been cancelled. (*ILLU*)

18 September 1902: Pinkerton Detective Mr. Leverton gets on the trail of Giuseppe Gorgiano in London. (*REDC*)

19 September 1902: Gennaro Lucca sends another secret message to Emilia Lucca via the agony columns of the *Daily Gazette*. (*REDC*)

19 September 1902: Baron Adelbert Gruner intended to take a trip from Liverpool on the *Ruritania*. (*ILLU*)

23 September 1902: Gennaro Lucca sends another secret message to Emilia Lucca via the agony columns of the *Daily Gazette*. (*REDC*)

24 September 1902: Concerned about her lodger being so secretive, Mrs. Warren consults Holmes. (*REDC*)

25 September 1902: Gennaro Lucca sends another secret message to Emilia Lucca via the agony columns of the *Daily Gazette*. (*REDC*)

25 September 1902 – 7 am: Mistaken for Gennaro Lucca by Giuseppe Gorgiano's men, Mr. Warren is abducted as he leaves his home. Realising their mistake, he is released an hour later. (*REDC*)

25 September 1902 – Afternoon: Holmes investigates what has been going on with Mrs. Warren's lodger. (*REDC*)

25 September 1902 – Evening: Holmes and Watson meet Mr. Leverton and Inspector Tobias Gregson and they discover the corpse of Giuseppe Gorgiano. Holmes solves the case and reveals all. (*REDC*)

October 1902: Violet de Merville was due to marry Baron Adelbert Gruner. (*ILLU*)

18 January 1903: James M. Dodd writes to Godfrey Emsworth's mother and receives an invitation to visit the following day and to stay the night. (*BLAN*)

19 January 1903 – Evening: James M. Dodd visits the Emsworth family home (Tuxbury Old Park). He sees the pale face of his friend Godfrey Emsworth through the window. (*BLAN*)

20 January 1903: James M. Dodd invites himself to stay one more night at Tuxbury Old Park. He then spends the day attempting to trace his friend, Godfrey Emsworth. When he is caught snooping by Colonel Emsworth that evening, he is ordered to leave first thing the following morning. (*BLAN*)

21 January 1903 – 8 am: After a sleepless night, James M. Dodd leaves Tuxbury Old Park with the intention of consulting Holmes. (*BLAN*)

21 January 1903 – Afternoon: James M. Dodd sends a letter to Holmes informing him of his intention to visit later the same day. He uses stationery he has stolen from Tuxbury Old Park. (*BLAN*)

21 January 1903: Holmes is visited at 221b by James M. Dodd, who asks for Holmes's assistance in tracing his missing army friend, Godfrey Emsworth. (*BLAN*)

Between 21 and 26 January 1903: Holmes deals with a commission from the Sultan of Turkey to avoid political consequences of the gravest kind. (*BLAN*)

Between 21 and 26 January 1903: Holmes is finishing up the case of the Abbey School, in which the Duke of Greyminster was deeply involved. Despite having abandoned Holmes for a wife, Watson assists enough to be able to privately publish an account of this case later on. (*BLAN*)

26 January 1903: Holmes, James M. Dodd, and Sir James Saunders travel to Tuxbury Old Place where Holmes reveals all and Sir James Saunders reveals that Godfrey Emsworth is merely suffering from ichthyosis. (*BLAN*)

Summer 1903: The events of "The Mazarin Stone" take place in one evening. At 7 pm, Watson arrives at 221b after a long absence. Holmes enlists his help springing a trap to catch Count Negretto Sylvius and Sam Merton and retrieve the Mazarin Stone which they stole. He then returns it to Lord Cantlemere. (*MAZA*)

June 1903: Professor Presbury becomes engaged to the daughter of Professor Morphy. (*CREE*)

June 1903: Professor Presbury goes on a fortnight's trip to Prague. He consults H. Lowestein, wanting to be more youthful. H. Lowestein suggests a course of injections of serum made from the glands of black-faced langurs. They make plans for the serum to be supplied to Professor Presbury through Lowestein's agent, A. Dorak. He returns home with a mysterious little wooden box containing his serum and needle. (*CREE*)

02 July 1903: Professor Presbury gets angry when Trevor Bennett touches his mysterious little wooden box. (*CREE*)

02 July 1903: The professor's dog, Roy, attacks Professor Presbury. This is due to the professor taking his dose of serum. (*CREE*)

11 July 1903: The professor's dog, Roy, attacks Professor Presbury. This is due to the professor taking his dose of serum. (*CREE*)

20 July 1903: The professor's dog, Roy, attacks Professor Presbury. This is due to the professor taking his dose of serum. Roy is banished to the stables. (*CREE*)

29 July 1903: There is trouble with Professor Presbury's behaviour. This is due to the professor taking his dose of serum. (*CREE*)

03 August 1903: Watson is finally allowed to write up and tell the events of "The Empty House." (*EMPT*)

07 August 1903: There is trouble with Professor Presbury's behaviour. This is due to the professor taking his dose of serum. (*CREE*)

16 August 1903: There is trouble with Professor Presbury's behaviour. This is due to the professor taking his dose of serum. (*CREE*)

26 August 1903: There is a period of excitement in Professor Presbury's behaviour. This is due to the professor taking his dose of serum. (*CREE*)

September 1903: "The Empty House" is first published publicly. (*EMPT*)

03 September 1903: There is trouble with Professor Presbury's behaviour. This is due to the professor taking his dose of serum. (*CREE*)

04 September 1903 – Night: Trevor Bennett witnesses Professor Presbury crawling around the house like a monkey. (*CREE*)

05 September 1903: Trevor Bennett sends Holmes some communication of his intention to consult at 221b regarding the mysterious behaviour of Professor Presbury. (*CREE*)

05 September 1903 – Night: Edith Presbury sees her father, Professor Presbury, outside her bedroom window climbing up the side of the house. (*CREE*)

06 September 1903 – Evening: Watson receives a telegram from Holmes summoning him to 221b. About half an hour later Trevor Bennett arrives and lays out the details of Professor Presbury's peculiar behaviour. (*CREE*)

06 September 1903 – Evening: Edith Presbury, the professor's daughter and Trevor Bennett's fiancée, arrives at 221b and adds her experiences to the evidence. (*CREE*)

07 September 1903 – Morning: Holmes and Watson visit Professor Presbury at his home in Camford. Professor Presbury angrily turns them away, so they take up residence at a nearby inn, The Chequers. Holmes telegrams for information from his new agent, Mercer. (*CREE*)

08 September 1903: Expecting no more trouble until 15 September 1903, Holmes and Watson return to London. (*CREE*)

14 September 1903 – Evening: Holmes and Watson get a train back to Camford. (*CREE*)

15 September 1903 – 12 am: Holmes and Watson stake out Professor Presbury's home. As predicted, the professor takes his dose and begins to act strangely. He taunts Roy, the dog, who slips his leash and attacks the Professor Presbury. After the professor is saved, Holmes reveals all. (*CREE*)

October 1903: "The Norwood Builder" is first published publicly. (*NORW*)

December 1903: "The Dancing Men" is first published publicly. (*DANC*)

December 1903: "The Solitary Cyclist" is first published publicly. (*SOLI*)

January 1904: "The Priory School" is first published publicly. (*PRIO*)

February 1904: "Black Peter" is first published publicly. (*BLAC*)

March 1904: "Charles Augustus Milverton" is first published publicly. (*CHAS*)

April 1904: "The Six Napoleons" is first published publicly. (*SIXN*)

June 1904: "The Three Students" is first published publicly. (*3STU*)

July 1904: "The Golden Pince-Nez" is first published publicly. (*GOLD*)

August 1904: "The Missing Three-Quarter" is first published publicly. (*MISS*)

September 1904: "The Abbey Grange" is first published publicly. (*ABBE*)

December 1904: "The Second Stain" is first published publicly. (*SECO*)

December 1904: By this time Holmes has retired to keep bees on the Sussex Downs. (*SECO*)

1905: Jack Woodley due to be released from prison. (*SOLI*)

1906: Ian Murdoch and Fitzroy McPherson reconcile their differences and become good friends. (*LION*)

21 and 22 July 1907: Storms of extraordinary violence occur across Britain and Ireland. (*LION*)

23 July 1907 – Morning: During a morning swim in the sea, Fitzroy McPherson is stung by *cyanea capillata*. He gets out of the water, gets partially dressed and tries to reach the main road for help. (*LION*)

23 July 1907 – Morning: Holmes and his friend Ian Murdoch encounter Fitzroy McPherson just as he is dying. (*LION*)

30 July 1907: Fitzroy McPherson's dog dies at the same spot as Fitzroy McPherson, and in the same way. (*LION*)

31 July 1907 – Morning: During a morning swim in the sea, Ian Murdoch is stung by *cyanea capillata*. He gets out of the water and manages to make his way to Holmes's retirement cottage where he is treated until he will survive. (*LION*)

31 July 1907 – Morning: Holmes's explains that Fitzroy McPherson and his dog were killed by *cyanea capillata*. With Inspector Bardle and Harold Stackhurst, Holmes goes to the site of their deaths and kills the *cyanea capillata*. (*LION*)

August 1908: "Wisteria Lodge" is first published publicly. (*WIST*)

December 1908: "The Bruce-Partington Plans" is first published publicly. (*BRUC*)

1910: Hugo Oberstein is due for release from prison. (*BRUC*)

1910: Von Bork moves into his English residence near Harwich. (*LAST*)

1910: Watson receives a telegram from Holmes requesting that Watson write up and publish the story of "The Devil's Foot," (*DEVI*)

06 May 1910: Death of King Edward VII. (*History*)

December 1910: "The Devil's Foot" is first published publicly. (*DEVI*)

March 1911: "The Red Circle" is first published publicly. (*REDC*)

22 June 1911: Coronation of King George V. (*History*)

December 1911: "Lady Frances Carfax" is first published publicly. (*LADY*)

1912: Holmes travels to Chicago where he disguises himself as an Irish-American called Altamont and embarks on a two-year mission to infiltrate a ring of German secret agents. (*LAST*)

November 1913: "The Dying Detective" is first published publicly. (*DYIN*)

28 July 1914: The assassination of Archduke Franz Ferdinand of Austria. (*History*)

01 August 1914: Von Bork's wife and household leave England to go to Flushing (*LAST*)

02 August 1914: Colonel Sebastian Moran is still alive. (*LAST*)

02 August 1914 – 12 pm: Pretending to be an agent of Von Bork called Altamont, Holmes telegraphs Von Bork to say he will arrive at Von Bork's with stolen naval signals that evening. (*LAST*)

02 August 1914 – 9 pm: Von Bork meets with Baron von Herling and they walk to Von Bork's English residence near Harwich. (*LAST*)

02 August 1914 – Late evening: At the Harwich home of Von Bork, Baron von Herling leaves, Holmes in his Altamont character arrives, captures Von Bork, reveals all and converses with Watson, who has been acting as Altamont's chauffeur. (*LAST*)

02 August 1914 – Late evening: Holmes expresses to Watson that he thinks this may be the last time they will be able to have a quiet talk. (*LAST*)

02 August 1914 – Late evening: Holmes and Watson drive back to London with Von Bork as a prisoner. (*LAST*)

03 August 1914: Martha reports to Holmes at Claridge's Hotel. (*LAST*)

04 August 1914: Great Britain enters World War I. (*History*)

September 1914: *The Valley of Fear* is first published publicly. (*VALL*)

September 1917: "His Last Bow" is first published publicly. (*LAST*)

11 November 1918: End of World War I. (*History*)

October 1921: "The Mazarin Stone" is first published publicly. (*MAZA*)

1922: Watson writes "How Watson Learned the Trick" for the library of Queen Mary's Dolls' House. (*Apocrypha*)

February 1922: "Thor Bridge" is first published publicly. (*THOR*)

March 1923: "The Creeping Man" is first published publicly. (*CREE*)

1924: "How Watson Learned the Trick" is first published publicly. (*Apocrypha*)

January 1924: "The Sussex Vampire" is first published publicly. (*SUSS*)

October 1924: "The Three Garridebs" is first published publicly. (*3GAR*)

November 1924: "The Illustrious Client" is first published publicly. (*ILLU*)

September 1926: "The Three Gables" is first published publicly. (*3GAB*)

October 1926: "The Blanched Soldier" is first published publicly. (*BLAN*)

November 1926: "The Lion's Mane" is first published publicly. (*LION*)

December 1926: "The Retired Colourman" is first published publicly. (*RETI*)

January 1927: "The Veiled Lodger" is first published publicly. (*VEIL*)

March 1927: "Shoscombe Old Place" is first published publicly. (*SHOS*)

07 July 1930: Watson's literary agent, Sir Arthur Ignatius Conan Doyle, dies. (*History*)

Undated Unpublished Cases

There are several unpublished cases which it is impossible to place meaningfully on a Holmesian timeline. These I list here with what limitations on date I can supply.

Between June 1876 and 1881: Holmes investigates the Tarleton murders. (*MUSG*)

Between June 1876 and 1881: Holmes investigates the case of Vamberry, the wine merchant. (*MUSG*)

Between June 1876 and 1881: Holmes investigates the adventure of the old Russian woman. (*MUSG*)

Between June 1876 and 1881: Holmes investigates the singular affair of the aluminium crutch. (*MUSG*)

Between June 1876 and 1881: Holmes is involved in the case of Ricoletti of the club-foot, and his abominable wife. (*MUSG*)

Sometime between June 1876 and March 1881: Holmes helps Mrs. Farintosh in a case concerned with an opal tiara. (*SPEC*)

Sometime between June 1876 and September 1887: Holmes proves Major Prendergast innocent of cheating at cards in the Tankerville Club scandal. (*FIVE*)

Sometime between June 1876 and October 1887: Lord Backwater is given cause to trust Holmes. (*NOBL*)

Sometime between June 1876 and October 1887: There is a similar case to "The Noble Bachelor" in Aberdeen. (*NOBL*)

Sometime between June 1876 and 19 November 1887: Holmes is engaged by the firm of Morrison, Morrison, and Dodd to solve the case of *Matilda Briggs*, a ship which is associated with the giant rat of Sumatra. (*SUSS*)

Sometime between June 1876 and 19 November 1887: Holmes is involved in a remarkable case involving a gila monster. (*SUSS*)

Sometime between June 1876 and July 1888: Holmes provides some slight service to Mrs. Cecil Forrester with her domestic complication. (*SIGN*)

Sometime between June 1854 and July 1888: Holmes knows a woman who is hanged for poisoning three little children for their insurance-money. (*SIGN*)

Sometime between June 1854 and July 1888: Holmes knows a repellent philanthropist who has spent nearly a quarter of a million upon the London poor. (*SIGN*)

Sometime between June 1876 and July 1888: Holmes assists the police in the Bishopgate jewel case. (*SIGN*)

Sometime between June 1876 and June 1889: Holmes locates the missing Mr. Etherege on behalf of his wife. (*IDEN*)

Sometime between June 1876 and August 1889: Holmes, Lestrade, and Aldridge are involved in The Bogus Laundry Affair. (*CARD*)

Sometime between March 1881 and September 1889: Holmes takes an interest in the case of Selden, the Notting Hill murderer. (*HOUN*)

Sometime before September 1889: The Anderson murders in North Carolina take place. They are analogous to the crimes in *The Hound of the Baskervilles*. This is not a case which Holmes was involved in. (*HOUN*)

Sometime between June 1876 and 24 September 1889: Holmes saves the good name of Wilson who works in a district messenger office. (*HOUN*)

Sometime between March 1881 and May 1891: Watson introduces the case of Colonel Warburton's madness to Holmes. (*ENGI*)

Sometime between March 1881 and 27 April 1895: Holmes and Watson catch Archie Stamford, the forger, near Farnham. (*SOLI*)

Sometime between June 1876 and 14 December 1897: Holmes is involved in a case which resulted in Henry Staunton being hanged. (*MISS*)

Sometime between March 1881 and June 1900: Holmes and Watson work on the dreadful business of the Abernetty family (which was first brought to Holmes's notice by the depth which the parsley had sunk into the butter upon a hot day). (*SIXN*)

Sometime before 1901: Baron Gruner murders his wife in the Splugen Pass, Prague. Holmes is not involved in the case, but does read about it. (*ILLU*)

Sometime before 1902: Count Sylvius is responsible for the death of Mrs. Harold so that he can inherit the Blymer Estate. Holmes was not involved in this case at the time. (*MAZA*)

Sometime before 1902: Count Sylvius is involved with Miss Minnie Warrender in a way which is somehow criminal. Holmes was not involved in this case at the time. (*MAZA*)

Sometime before 02 September 1902: Colonel Damery negotiates with Sir George Lewis over the Hammerford Will case. It is unclear whether Holmes is involved in the case. (*ILLU*)

Sometime before 02 September 1902: Baron Gruner has Le Brun, a French agent, beaten and crippled for life. Holmes is not involved in the case. (*ILLU*)

Sometime before 18 September 1902: Mr. Leverton, of Pinkerton's American Agency, distinguishes himself in the Long Island Cave mystery. This is not a case Holmes was involved in, but he did show an interest in it. (*REDC*)

Sometime between March 1881 and September 1903: Holmes fails to solve the case of Mr. James Phillimore, who, stepping back into his own house to get his umbrella, was never more seen in this world. (*THOR*)

Sometime between March 1881 and September 1903: Holmes fails to solve the case of the cutter *Alicia*, which sailed one spring morning into a small patch of mist from where she never again emerged. (*THOR*)

Sometime between March 1881 and September 1903: Holmes fails to solve the case of Isadora Persano, the well-known journalist and duellist, who was found stark staring mad with a match box in front of him which contained a remarkable worm said to be unknown to science. (*THOR*)

Sometime between March 1881 and September 1903: Holmes and Watson are involved in a case concerning a politician, a lighthouse, and a trained cormorant. (*VEIL*)

Sometime between June 1876 and 1912: Holmes saves Count Von und Zu Grafenstein from a murder plot by the Nihilist Klopman. (*LAST*)

THE JAY FINLEY CHRIST
ABBREVIATIONS

AN OUTLINE OF THE STANDARD
HOLMESIAN STORY ABBREVIATIONS

The Canonical Stories are typically abbreviated using the four letter system created by Jay Finley Christ. I have used them myself in this chronology. For the uninitiated, here is an alphabetical list of the abbreviations and the stories they represent:

ABBE – The Abbey Grange
BERY – The Beryl Coronet
BLAC – Black Peter
BLAN – The Blanched Soldier
BLUE – The Blue Carbuncle
BOSC – The Boscombe Valley Mystery
BRUC – The Bruce-Partington Plans
CARD – The Cardboard Box
CHAS – Charles Augustus Milverton
COPP – The Copper Beeches
CREE – The Creeping Man
CROO – The Crooked Man
DANC – The Dancing Men
DEVI – The Devil's Foot
DYIN – The Dying Detective
EMPT – The Empty House
ENGR – The Engineer's Thumb
FINA – The Final Problem
FIVE – The Five Orange Pips
GLOR – The *Gloria Scott*
GOLD – The Golden Pince-Nez

GREE – The Greek Interpreter
HOUN – The Hound of the Baskervilles
IDEN – A Case of Identity
ILLU – The Illustrious Client
LADY – The Disappearance of Lady Frances Carfax
LAST – His Last Bow
LION – The Lion's Mane
MAZA – The Mazarin Stone
MISS – The Missing Three-Quarter
MUSG – The Musgrave Ritual
NAVA – The Naval Treaty
NOBL – The Noble Bachelor
NORW – The Norwood Builder
PRIO – The Priory School
REDC – The Red Circle
REDH – The Red-Headed League
REIG – The Reigate Squires
RESI – The Resident Patient
RETI – The Retired Colourman
SCAN – A Scandal in Bohemia
SECO – The Second Stain
SHOS – Shoscombe Old Place
SIGN – The Sign of the Four
SILV – Silver Blaze
SIXN – The Six Napoleons
SOLI – The Solitary Cyclist
SPEC – The Speckled Band
STOC – The Stockbroker's Clerk
STUD – A Study in Scarlet
SUSS – The Sussex Vampire
THOR – The Problem of Thor Bridge
3GAB – The Three Gables
3GAR – The Three Garridebs
3STU – The Three Students
TWIS – The Man with the Twisted Lip
VALL – The Valley of Fear
VEIL – The Veiled Lodger
WIST – Wisteria Lodge
YELL – The Yellow Face

BIBLIOGRAPHY

Books:

Bradshaw, George. *Bradshaw's Rail Times 1850: for Great Britain and Ireland*. Middleton Press, 2012.

Doyle, Arthur Conan, and William Stuart Baring-Gould. *The Annotated Sherlock Holmes: the Four Novels and the Fifty-Six Short Stories Complete*. Clarkson N. Potter, 1979.

Doyle, Arthur Conan, et al. *The New Annotated Sherlock Holmes*. W.W. Norton, 2007.

Tracy, Jack. *The Encyclopaedia Sherlockiana: or, A Universal Dictionary of the State of Knowledge of Sherlock Holmes and His Biographer John H. Watson*. New English Library, 1978.

Utechin, Nicholas. *Sherlock Holmes at Oxford*. Robert Dugdale, 1981.

Websites:

Met Office. "Monthly Weather Report." *Met Office*, Met Office, 15 Oct. 2018, www.metoffice.gov.uk/learning/library/archive-hidden-treasures/monthly-weather-report

Archive, The British Newspaper. "Discover History As It Happened." *Register | British Newspaper Archive*, Illustrated London News Group, www.britishnewspaperarchive.co.uk

Royal Albert Hall, "Performance History and Archive." www./catalogue.royalalberthall.com

CPSIA information can be obtained
at www.ICGtesting.com
Printed in the USA
LVHW091319131219
640409LV00001B/156/P

9 781479 444335